AF478540

Les Triplés

Your Gift Problems Are Solved

** I Am Not My Mother*

** Les Triplés*

** You Have No New Messages*

** Budd's Epiphany*

Daniel Plucinski's new novels may be purchased by
e-mail request to:dplucinski@frostburg.edu
Type message:"Send me a book order form."

And I shall send you a purchase order.

Les Triplés

Daniel Plucinski

Shaffer Publishing

For further information, please contact:

Shaffer Publishing
Frostburg, Maryland
dplucinski@frostburg.edu

Book design by:

Arbor Books, Inc.
19 Spear Road, Suite 202
Ramsey, NJ 07446
www.arborbooks.com

Printed in Canada

Les Triplés
Daniel Plucinski

1. Title 2. Author 3. Fiction

Library of Congress Control Number: 2005909778
ISBN: 0-9767598-1-0

Acknowledgements

I would like to thank Dr. Judy Pula of Frostburg State University for her excellent contribution as proofreader. Dr. Gerard Wojnar and Hania Merrill provided the Polish translations.

Chapter I

"Ouch!" I cried as another thorn pricked me and pulled a thread out of the weave of my white tee-shirt. I looked down at the nearly full quart basket of black raspberries. I thought, "A few more berries and I will be done." I was tired of getting "jagger" scratches. But I was motivated to complete the quart so that I could realize the big payoff.

No one was home at the first house I approached. An elderly Italian woman at the second house answered my knock. She glanced skeptically at my berries in the usual Italian way to pose the most advantageous bargaining position as she asked about my price. "Twenty-five cents," I replied. "It is a good price. The fruit market charges thirty-nine."

From the shadows of the hallway, a young girl came to the door. I recognized her as Angelin. She was eleven years old and in the next grade after mine at school. I thought the old woman was her grandmother with whom Angelin visited during the summer. The kids on the playground made fun of Angelin because she had an obvious under-bite. The kids called her "cash register" because her lower jaw jutted out like a cash register drawer.

The lady said that she would take the berries. She went back into the house to fetch her pocketbook. As the lady moved out of her hearing distance, I shyly glanced at Angelin and said, "Hi."

"Hi Daniel," she relied. I was surprised that Angelin, as an older pupil, knew my name. She pronounced it correctly as dun-yell. I speculated that she knew me as the milk boy. At 10:30 every morning in school, I dutifully went down to the basement and loaded from the cooler a designated number of six-ounce glass bottles of milk into crates for delivery to each classroom. I hauled each crate up one flight of stairs for grades one, two and three. Grades four through six required two flights of stairs. The kids were always glad to see me break the boredom of study. A bottle of milk cost six cents. For the labor, my bottle was free. I never told Mum that I got my milk for free. Each week she gave me thirty cents milk money, and I squirreled it into a canvas bank pouch with heavy duty drawstrings at the top. I kept the money pouch in a cardboard cigar box. I had painstakingly used a screwdriver to hand drill a hole into the lid and another hole near the top of the front panel of the box. I fished the prong of an open padlock through the two holes. When the cigar box was padlocked, I felt that my fortune was secure. After accumulating five dollars from milk money and other business ventures, I deposited the funds into a savings account at the bank to earn interest on the increasing balance.

"Where did you get the blackberries?" Angelin asked.

"Along the natural gas line trails in the woods. Berry bushes like the sunlight provided by the clear cut along the gas line. There is a boatload of berries out there. By the way, they are black raspberries, not blackberries. The blackberries are larger and will not ripen for another month."

"Will you be selling them, too."

"I expect I will."

The lady returned with the quarter. When she extended a hand to take the basket, I informed her that "the basket is not included. That is the only basket I got. I need it to collect more berries. Since a thorn pulled a thread on my tee shirt, my mum will yell at me if I do not also bring home a carton full of berries."

The lady took the basket from me and handed it to Angelin. She commanded Angelin, "Dump them berries into the small pot sitting on the stove. Pour water on them and let'em soak."

"Why are you soaking them?" I asked with curiosity. "That will make them mushy. What is the problem? Are you worried that the berries lack enough chemical pesticides to kill you?"

The lady shrugged as if she really did not wish to talk about her thoughts but said, "You don't know what touched the berries in them woods. Animals could've … done their business on them."

"The animals are too small to do their business on the berry bushes," I assured her.

"What about them bears and deers?"

"There are no bears around here and very few deer." I replied

I knew I was supposed to say "thank you" to the old woman, but I did not. My parents always used to poke me in the ribs to induce me to say thank you to people, especially to my grandmother, but I seldom did. I felt too awkward saying thank you, especially when a person gave me something I really did not want anyway. The words seemed unnatural, fake and phony. I sometimes gagged on the words because they were so dishonest when I uttered them. The old woman did not have to buy the raspberries if she did not want them or did not like the price. Why should I have thanked her when she got what she wanted? If she had not wanted them, I could have sold the berries to someone else. We both got what we wanted out of the transaction. So, why should either one have felt obligated to thank the other? Would it not have been more honest if we had simply said "so long"?

As I departed my customers' house, I kept my right hand in the pants pocket where I had deposited the quarter. It felt large while I turned the quarter over and over again within my fingers. I savored the satisfaction of being a man of means. I returned to the woods. I was bored with berry picking, but the sense of self-importance derived from delivering food to my home was a motivator. I also looked forward to the berry pies Mum would bake. Unfortunately for my mother, I avoided most other chores at home. Washing dishes and redding up my bedroom by making new piles out of old piles of stuff just did not seem to accomplish anything of value. But delivering berries or freshly caught fish was an activity with substance that brought me recognition.

๛๛๛

I had always had entrepreneurial proclivity. At four years old, I washed old pennies and rubbed them on a rag to give them a shine. Targeting the residencies of little old ladies, I went to each house proffering to exchange my shiny penny for two of their old pennies. My enterprise was a huge success and a great funding source for penny candy at the corner mom-and-pop grocery. Upon discovering my enterprise, my mum ended the venture because it embarrassed her.

On the way home from the woods with the last quart of raspberries for the day, I passed Angelin's grandmother's house. Angelin was sitting on a three-person-wide swing on the front porch, playing dolls with another girl named Joanie. She was my age and a classmate who would start fifth grade with me at Wilson School in September. Joanie had teeth growing over her front teeth from high up in the gums of her upper mouth. It looked like her mouth was too small or she had too many teeth. She also had a raspy voice and limp, stringy hair. All of the kids at school made fun of her. Having caught sight of me, Angelin came racing towards me with Joanie following. "Do you have another basketful of berries?" Angelin yelled. Instinctively, I glanced around to make sure that no one, especially other guys, saw me talking to girls. I slowed and shuffled sideways as I proudly held out the testament to my worthiness. "Are you gonna sell them, too?" Joanie asked when the girls had caught up to me.

"No," I replied. "These are going home."

"Can we have some?" Angelin asked with her hand extended like a miniature steam shovel.

"No." I jerked the carton away from their reach. I was not greedy. But I did not want to have diminished the splendor of the display when I would later present the quart to Mum. My berries were similar in importance to me like Mum's Christmas spice cookies were to her. The cookies were always made for someone else—for company. They were never made for me, except for some cookies at the corner of the baking sheet that were burnt or broken. I used to pray for such a casualty… "Why are you following me?" I asked the girls.

"Angelin told me that you get your berries in the woods. We want you to take us for a walk in the woods," Joanie said. Angelin glanced at Joanie from the corners of her eyes as if she was not comfortable with Joanie's proposition, but Angelin did not express an objection.

The idea of having company on my adventures in the woods was appealing. However, I said, "Your mum and dad would never let you go into the woods."

"Why are you allowed to go into the woods?" Joanie asked.

"My mum has no idea how far I go when I go for a hike. My

parents think that I pick the berries at the edge of the field by the water tanks."

"OK, then we'll tell our parents that we're going to play with a friend down the street," Angelin said. "Then we'll go with you."

I pondered the risk involved with the proposal. I enjoyed hours of unsupervised freedom unheard of by every kid my age. I always returned home on time for dinner. Miraculously, I never returned with dirty clothes, although I frequently washed mud from my clothes and sneakers in a stream and wore them wet for hours until they dried. Years later, when my sister questioned the reason for the total freedom granted to me when I was a child, my mother responded that "with five kids, you can't worry about them all. Daniel could always take care of himself." I imagined a parent of either Angelin or Joanie panicking when the girls could not be found. Neighbors would be enlisted to search for them. When I would emerge from the woods with the girls, I would be in deep trouble, my grant of freedom in jeopardy. "I do not think that it would be a good idea for me to take you into the woods," I decreed.

"If you take us, I'll convince my grandma to buy another basket of berries from you," Angelin offered.

"I have no problem selling berries. That is not giving me any-thing." I turned to walk away.

"I'll convince Grandma to hire you to shovel her sidewalks when it snows," Angelin anteed up.

Whoa, that attracted my attention. A snowfall creates a treasure trove of cash opportunity for anyone with a shovel. But people were reluctant to hire a ten-year-old, even though I was more diligent than the hotshot older kids, albeit a little slower. I pivoted and walked back-wards away from the girls as I said, "I will think about it."

No one was in the kitchen when I arrived at home. The bathroom door was closed, so I presumed someone, perhaps my mum, was occu-pying it. I could hardly believe my great luck. I placed the carton atop the kitchen table and quickly tiptoed to the bedroom that I shared with my four-year-old brother, Kenny. He was napping. I quietly opened my dresser drawer. I pulled my tee shirt over my head and hid it underneath the clean clothes. I thought, "I will wait until the coast is clear. Then I will sneak the tee shirt downstairs to the cellar and put it into the middle of the laundry pile. Mum probably will not see the pulled thread. When the shirt is hung to dry on the clothes line, I will point to it and let Mum think that it was damaged by the washing machine."

When I returned to the kitchen, Mum was there. She whispered, "I gotta go down and get a load of laundry."

A few minutes after Mum had gone, my dad came into the kitchen from the backyard where he had been spraying the apple trees with insecticide. He asked me where Mum was. I replied, "She went down to the cellar."

Dad looked at me as if I had uttered a profanity. He angrily said, "She's no *she*. She's your mother. You must say, 'My mother went downstairs', not *she*." I was surprised, upset and resentful. I did not take criticism well, especially when I made such extraordinary effort to not offend anyone. I felt a sense of entrapment. If I had observed in social discourse a ban against the use of a pronoun when referring to one's mother, then perhaps an accusatory tone by my father would have been warranted. But I had never before heard anyone eschew the word *she*. I referred to my teachers using the word *she*, and they were a lot older than my mother. Had my dad previously warned me about the improper address, then he could have justifiably berated me. He made me feel like I was a bad boy because I should have known, without forewarning, that the use of *she* when referring to my mother was disrespectful. Maybe Adam and Eve used the expression *she*. It must have been part of the original sin that I was learning about in catechism. With original sin, you are automatically guilty, even though you did not do anything wrong.

⁂

Angelin and Joanie wore skirts for their first excursion into the woods. To not discourage their excitement, I did not tell them of my prediction that their unprotected legs would contract poison *ivory* and ticks. We hiked through woodland of oak and locust that teemed with squirrels. The girls marveled when I pointed to the large squirrel nests formed of leaves at the confluence of branches. On a mud flat, I showed them the dual imprints of deer hooves. We found a deep-shelled land tortoise. After much coaxing, Joanie and I convinced Angelin to pick it up. I cautioned her to hold the tortoise away from her body because a picked-up tortoise tends to pee out of fright. Joanie found a large feather. It looked like a pen used by those sissy-looking guys who wrote the Declaration of Independence. Joanie slid the feather under the belt of her skirt, claiming it as her trophy.

We crossed a small spring. Seized by a pioneering spirit, I suggested that we build a dam that would create a pond. We hunted for large flat rocks along the spring bed. We stacked the rocks in the flow, impeding it. After raising the impoundment a mere two inches, the dam sprung leaks. Shaping my left hand in the form of a paddle, I placed it into the spring upstream from the dam and shoveled silt against the dam. The improved seal raised the pond level eight inches. I took off my shoes and socks and rolled up the cuffs of my pants. Wading into the pool, I scooped handfuls of silt from the upper end of the pool and threw the silt onto the banks. When finished, I had excavated holes over a foot in depth. I told the girls that I would go fishing in Beaver Run within the next couple of days to catch some bluegills and that I would carry the fish in a bucketful of water and stock the fish in our pool. The thought—of creating an environment and propagating a specie in it—captivated the girls' imaginations.

I stood up and unzipped my pants in preparation to take a leak. I halted the process as I realized that that day was not like any other day. I could not choose to go just anywhere. Some law somewhere forbade me from engaging in the most common act. I quickly pivoted my back towards the girls as I zipped up. My eyes searched for underbrush that would sufficiently conceal me. As I pushed through the brush, the girls giggled as they sang the schoolyard chant heard during recess, "We know where you're going. We know what you're doing."

Emerging from the brush, I said, "I better get you back home before your folks get suspicious." I started walking expecting the girls to follow.

Angelin hollered to me, "Isn't the way back that way?" She pointed to the right.

"No, Vandergrift is in that direction, west," I replied.

"How can you be sure? How do you know that way is west?"

"Would you believe because I have spent my whole life in these woods? Look at that tree. See the moss? Moss grows on the north side of trees where it will not get dried out by the sun. Look at this tree over here … and that tree and even that rock. The moss is growing on the same side, north. Now, face the same way the moss faces. That is north. Point your left arm straight out to the left. You are pointing west."

"But what if you are in the middle of a field with no trees?" Joanie asked.

"If you have at least a little bit of sun, and if you know the time of day, you can determine direction. Turn your back to the sun so that you are facing your shadow. If it was one a'clock, we would be facing north."

"Isn't that supposed to happen at high noon?" Angelin said sarcastically.

"We are in daylight savings time, which pushes the north shadow to one a'clock."

"It can't be one a'clock already," Angelin said

"It is 11:35," I said. "From here you can hear the bells of Saint Ignatius in Apollo. It rings one bell on the half-hour. It rang about five minutes ago. It was faint, but did you hear it?"

"I didn't ear any bell," Angelin said. Joanie shrugged *no*.

"I did," I said. "But I was listening for it. It is too late to be ten-thirty and too early for twelve-thirty. It must be eleven-thirty."

"So what's the big deal about eleven-thirty?" Angelin groaned.

"Since we are an hour and a half earlier than the sun being directly south, then it is a little east of due south. That means that our shadows are pointing a little west of north. We need to adjust a little right to face north." Angelin and Joanie glanced at each other and rolled their eyes. I stepped behind Angelin and looked over her right shoulder to see her shadow. Placing my hands on her shoulders, I pivoted her body slightly to the right so that her line of sight would form a side to an imaginary cheese wedge with her shadow casting the other side. "There, you are facing north. Now point your left hand straight out to the left. That is west."

"That's the same direction we pointed to when we faced the same direction as the moss," Joanie observed. "Are you a scout?"

"No," I said.

"Did your dad teach you about finding your direction?" Joanie asked.

"No."

"Well, then how do you know all this stuff?"

"I don't know why I know it. I do not remember ever learning it. I have just always known it. I spend a lot of time looking at maps."

To return home we had to climb a ridge and descend the other side. The soil had been worn from the path that we needed to descend, leaving loose, slippery shale chips. I demonstrated my expertise at sitting on my haunches with my arms clasped around my knees as I skated down the steep slope. The girls hesitated a long time until Angelin, a year older and a little braver, attempted the slide, screaming the whole way. Fearing abandonment, Joanie soon followed. She did not, however, balance her weight over her feet. She fell back, sliding half of the slope on her *dupa*. It would have been bad enough if she had been wearing jeans. Her skirt rode up exposing her bum and the back of her thighs to the abrasiveness of the trail. When she came to rest, there was a surreal moment of silence as Joanie recovered her senses. She screamed in agony as she sat on the mogul of dirt collected by the plowing action of trail users. Angelin and I lifted her to her feet. Angelin pulled up the back of Joanie's skirt, revealing the streamers of bloody scrapes. I empathized with Joanie's feeling of pain. Two months earlier, I had fallen from my bike onto a cindered alley. I wanted to relieve Joanie's pain. So, I did something I had never before done with anyone. I hugged her. My family was not a huggy family. I felt her chest pant to the rhythms of her sobs. I continued holding her. Even as Joanie's sobs abated, I continued to hold her because I liked it. I whispered to her, "Do you think that you are ready to go?"

"It hurts," Joanie whimpered.

"I know it hurts," I whispered.

"What are we going to do?" Angelin asked in a mild panic.

"Pick her skirt up again," I requested. I looked at poor Joanie's raw wounds and said, "We do not have any choice. We are in the woods. When you are hurt in the woods, you walk home."

"But it hurts."

"I know it hurts. But you are not too hurt to walk. It is just painful to walk."

Joanie whimpered, "But it hurts real bad. What am I going to tell my mummy?"

"You are not going to tell anyone anything," I said firmly. "If you tell your folks, they will not let you out of your backyard for the rest of the summer." I looked at Joanie's lower legs with the skirt in its normal position. The injury was not evident. "You will walk into your house and go straight to your room. You get a clean pair of underwear and your softest pajamas. You go to the bathroom and wash your bum and legs. It will sting like hell, but you have to do it. I would suggest dabbing on some iodine, but you would faint from the pain. Slowly ease your PJ's on. Take the torn undies back to your room and bury it where no one will find it. Go downstairs and get something to eat. Sit on the ends of chairs so you will not rub your booboo."

"My folks will want to know why I'm wearing PJ's and acting so funny."

"Tell them that you were stung on the leg by a bumblebee and that you want to wear something soft. Do what I say, and three days from now you will be laughing about it. We will always remember today. But as far as your folks know, it never happened. By the way, sometime when no one is looking, slip the torn undies into the bottom of the trash bag."

Joanie bravely took the first of thousands of painful steps.

Chapter II

The clunking sound emanating from the brass knockers on the front door surprised Mum, Kenny and me. We rarely had visitors, never at seven-thirty on a Saturday morning. My little brother, Kenny, and I were in the kitchen eating a crisped cereal floating in milk. Mum exited the kitchen to answer the door at the far end of the parlor. I would have answered the knock if it was at the kitchen door, but I was not allowed to enter the parlor. Mum returned to the kitchen staring at me with a smirk on her face. She cocked her head to the side and placed her hands on her hips as she announced, "There are two girls outside who want to know if Daniel can come out to play." A deep flush instantaneously rolled across my face. No one in my family had ever seen me talk to a girl before. Neither my parents nor my grandparents ever exhibited any romantic interests. While I had no romantic interest in Angelin and Joanie, I was embarrassed by the appearance of an interaction between me and a girl, let alone two. The girls surprised me. The idea that they would have actually come to my house never occurred to me.

I went out the door to the back porch where Mum had sent Angelin and Joanie. "What are you doing here?" I huffed. The girls glanced at each other, surprised by the alien demeanor from the boy with whom they had built a dam with such camaraderie the day before. "How are your legs?" I asked Joanie.

Joanie grimaced and replied, "They hurt."

"Do they hurt when you are standing, like right now?"

"No, but they hurt when I sit," Joanie replied.

"Let me see them."

"I'm not letting you look up my dress."

"You did yesterday," I retorted.

"That was an emergency, and I was hurt. Besides, we were in the woods where nobody would see us." Joanie warily surveyed my neighbors' viewing perspectives of the porch. She pulled up her dress and bent forward slightly at the waist. I snickered at her immodesty after such protestation. I kneeled on one knee and closely examined her upper thighs. They were pink and scabbing with no signs of infection.

I cautioned her, "Soon the booboo will start itching like a sunburn, but do not scratch it, or it will become infected and scarred."

"Who do you think you are, a doctor?" Angelin quipped.

"When it comes to cuts and scrapes, I have more experience than any doctor." Turning to Joanie, I said, "I bet you will never want to go into the woods again."

"Oh no, I love the woods. I had a great time yesterday … well, until I slid on my bum. I want to go again, but next time I'm wearing pants."

"Then let's go today," I said without meaning it.

"No, not today. Give me time to heal. Besides, we have plans for later on. Angelin has a free pass to the matinee. Why don't you come with us?"

{*Good gravy,*} I thought. {*I would be a sissy's sissy, if I was seen going to a movie with girls. And I would be seen because everyone went to the Saturday matinee.*} "What's playing?" I asked.

"*The Mummy's Scream,*" Angelin projected while making her eyes grow large.

"I thought mummies did not make any sound, except some muffled noises," I mumbled with my hand over my mouth. "How much?"

"Fifteen cents," Joanie replied, displaying two nickels and five pennies.

{*Fifteen cents!*}, I thought. {*That was half of a week's milk allowance that I had banked yesterday, sixty percent of the profits from a quart of berries for which I would spend a whole morning picking and walking to and from the woods.*} I said, "I will go if you give me the free pass."

"No way," Angelin declared.

"I did not think you would buy the idea," I said. "To be fair, though, I think we should all pay the same amount, ten cents."

"How do you figure ten cents?" Angelin asked.

"Two fifteen-cent admissions plus one free pass. That is thirty cents divided among the three of us. You give me the free pass, and I will give each of you a nickel. I am out ten cents. Joanie gets to keep one of her nickels, so she is spending only ten cents of her own money. And you have to come up with ten cents of your own money to add to the nickel I give you."

"I don't like the idea," Angelin protested.

"I think it's a good idea," Joanie said. "It's fair. I would share a pass with you if I had one."

"Then it is settled," I proclaimed. "A two-to-one majority has voted that we share equally in the admission charge."

"But it's my free pass."

తింతింతిం

I had to grab Angelin by the arm to restrain her from walking down the aisle any closer to the theater screen. I explained, "We are almost beyond the edge of the balcony. Go ahead, take a few more steps and look up." Joanie and Angelin walked a few steps and saw the balcony full of kids hollering and bouncing in their seats. "As soon as the lights go out, the people down here and in front of the balcony are going to get bombarded with popcorn, pop cups and wads of used chewing gum."

"Oooooh," the girls chorused.

Angelin chanted as she slightly brushed her hand over Joanie's hair, "Gum full of spit getting into your hair." Joanie screamed and flailed her hands to bat away Angelin's intrusion. Angelin entered the row just behind the edge of the balcony. Joanie went to follow, but I clutched her arm and withheld her. I whispered to her, "No, I am sitting in the middle." I gently pulled her back into the aisle, and I stepped forward. I hoped the seating order was not a big deal to Joanie. But it was a big deal to me. During my whole life, my two older sisters forced me to sit beside our grandfather, Dziadzi (Judg—ee) during holiday meals. Dziadzi was cranky and complained a lot. His breath stank of chewing tobacco, and he was gassy and frequently cut loose SBD's. My older sisters did not want to sit beside Dziadzi. So they maneuvered to force me to always have to sit beside him, based on the rationalization, according to my sisters, that I looked like him. The main reason I had been forced to sit beside Dziadzi was because my sisters were older than I and used that advantage to boss me around. I vowed to never again be subjected to a seating arrangement by default to someone else's whim. That day, I felt like sitting between Joanie and Angelin.

The movie was as ridiculous as I had anticipated. The mummy had a gimpy leg that he dragged behind him as he walked. Even my grandmother, Babci (Bub-chi), could have run rings around that mummy. The mummy chased a blond lady who wore a sweater revealing a chest twice the size of her waist. The young lady could have walked faster than the mummy's top speed. But she did the only thing that could have given the mummy a chance of catching her. While running away, the lady tripped over a root in the path and twisted her ankle. The lady started screaming as she sat on the ground. The mummy took forever to get to the lady. All the time, the lady just sat there and kept screaming. If a mummy were chasing me, I think I would have gotten up and sprinted out of there, even with a gimpy ankle. As the mummy got closer, Joanie and Angelin started screaming. Both clasped my forearms and dug their nails into my biceps. So, I started to scream, too. Perhaps, sitting in the middle was not a good idea.

I had requested the girls bring their library cards so that we could stop at the library after the movie. The library was next door to the Casino Theater. "Why are we going to the library?" Joanie asked.

"Since we are already here, we might as well go in for a while," I said. "They have a book I want to take out."

"Which one?" Joanie asked.

"I have it written on a piece of paper … Here it is, *The Catcher in the Rye*."

"That's a strange title. What's it about?" Joanie asked.

"I don't know. The library has just made it available after years of banning it. I want to read it to see what the big deal is about."

"If it has been banned, then they don't want us to read it," Angelin said. "It must be about sex."

"It must be," I said. "I just do not understand why everyone makes such a big frick'n deal about the different ways men and ladies go to the bathroom. So what!" Joanie nodded her agreement.

An astonished grin swept across Angelin's face as she looked back and forth between Joanie and me. Angelin asked, "So you think that the only thing about sex concerns the different ways we pee?"

"There is more?" I asked.

"What about making babies?"

"She's right," Joanie confirmed. "Only women can have babies."

"But how are babies made?" Angelin prodded.

"Mummies make babies in their bellies." Joanie answered.

"But what makes mummies start to have a baby?" Angelin asked. There was silence. Angelin turned to me and said, "Come on, hotshot, you're the guy who knows everything. What makes a lady start to grow a baby?"

I drew in a deep breath as I pondered. "When a man and a lady are married for a while, … God, or maybe the Holy Ghost, visits the wife while she is sleeping and sprinkles holy powder on her that makes a baby start to grow."

"Yea, like the baby Jesus to Mary," Joanie beamed.

Angelin burst into laughter and said, "But Mary was a virgin when she gave birth. Do you know what a virgin is?"

Joanie and I glanced at each other. Joanie shrugged an I-don't-know gesture. I haltingly responded, "Well … ah … a virgin is a very sacred person, so sacred that the honor is given only to the Mother of Jesus who was anointed with virgin olive oil. Olive oil and olive branches were symbols of respect in biblical times."

"You're an amazing direction finder, but it's refreshing to see that you don't know everything," Angelin snickered.

"I don't think you have to be a sacred person to be a virgin," Joanie said. "I heard my mum say that my aunt was a virgin, and I guarantee that she's not sacred."

"Calling a person a virgin is just something people say," I explained, "just like when they call someone they know a saint, even though that person never met the pope."

We entered the library and went to the literature stacks. We scanned the latter part of the alphabet, looking for Salinger, J.D. Angelin stretched on her tippy-toes to grasp the book. She gave me *The Catcher in the Rye.* I retrieved my library card from my back pocket as we walked to the checkout counter. When the volunteer librarian observed the Polish name on my library card, he declared, "Good Irish name." The comment annoyed me. It was mildly nifty the first time I had heard it years ago. But by the ninety-seventh time, I grew weary of hearing "Good Irish name" whenever an Anglo saw or heard a Polish name. To make matters worse, the librarian followed up with the second most common cliché of the period by saying "I worked in the mill with a Polish fella. Good man, he was a really good man, first rate."

I projected a visage of amazement and said, "Wow, no kidding, you actually met a good one?" I partially regretted having made the reply. The librarian made the statement with good intentions. He did not know that I had heard it said dozens of times before. I guess I just resented the condescension, the implication that a patronizing expression of approval by a real American was necessary to contrast against a universally held low opinion of the Poles.

Angelin had been right. The librarian refused to let me borrow the book. It must have contained a lot of sex—you know—people getting undressed and rolling over each other for some weird reason.

Chapter III

"Let me go," Kent cried as he vainly squirmed to free himself from Pooza's grasp. My church was too small to have a regular school, so I had to attend an all-day catechism summer school for two weeks during June. Nuns were imported from other parishes to help the priest with the instruction. During the morning recess of the first day, most of the boys were in the grassy yard beside the church, threatening to beat up Kent Worthington. "Why do you want to beat me up?" Kent pleaded.

"Because you're not Polish," Pooza answered.

"My mother is Polish. I'm half Polish."

"OK," Kazik (Kuh-zjik) said, "we'll give you only half a beating. Honestly, with a name like yours, we should beat'cha up every day even if you were a hundred percent Polish."

Kent stomped on Pooza's right toe and wiggled out of his grasp. Kent bolted across the yard with five classmates in pursuit. They caught and subdued him at mid-yard. To Kent's credit, he did not cry for help. Hania (Hon-ya—girl) said to me, "Daniel, you better make them stop."

"Why should I? Everyone is having such a good time. You do not believe they would really hurt him, do you?"

"Should we give him the gas attack?" Jabo yelled to me as if my assent was important.

I said to Pooza who stood beside me, "Do you think you can work one out?" That was a stupid question. Pooza always had the capability. I waived a hand in a gesture that conveyed, "Why not." Pooza grinned and walked towards the assemblage. The boys held Kent on the ground, flat on his back. Pooza slid the back of his pants down to uncover his bum. Pooza did not have to slide his pants too far down because half of his crack was exposed all of the time anyway. Pooza lowered his crack to an inch from Kent's face and delivered the lethal fumes.

"That's disgusting … That's … that's," Hania burst out laughing. "I think I'd rather get beaten up. Why do you guys do that?"

"Oh, it is just a sort of … an initiation."

"Initiation to what, summer catechism?"

Looking back at Pooza, I said to Hania, "Pooza is a true work of art. Take a good look because someday he will be your husband." I covered my head with my arms as Hania slapped me with both hands rapidly and repeatedly.

After being released, Kent fled to the far edge of the churchyard. He stopped just long enough to yell, "Oh yea? … Well … Your mothers wear combat boots." Pooza made a two-step feint towards Kent who darted up the hill into the woods. The scene was comical because Pooza could not catch the gimpy mummy in the movie, let alone the swift footed Kent.

Kent barely got back in time for the resumption of instruction being held in a meeting room in the basement of the church. The priest dictated to us the list of the seven sacraments. The last sacrament was *extreme unction*. But the priest slurred the words, making them sound like *extra monkshin*. Kazik whispered, "Daniel, what is monkshin?"

"I do not know," I whispered back. "Maybe it is something that monks do. Whatever it is, if you do an extra amount over the normal amount of monkshin, you get credit for another sacrament."

"Maybe I should ask Father," Kazik suggested.

"Don't be stupid," chorused Jabo, Hania and Kasia (Kuh-sha—girl).

"Look," I explained to Kazik, "we do not have to know what any of this means. We will be tested only on the ability to recite the list of the seven sacraments. So, just write it down, extra monkshin."

The priest had us line up so that Sister Theresa could lead us out of the basement and up into the church. We sat in the first three pews in the front. We sang, "Tantum, ergo sacramentum …" When we finished, a man came to the door and motioned to Sister Theresa. She told us she would return shortly, and she excused herself.

"Why do we sing in Latin?" Kent whispered. "I don't know what any of these words mean."

"You're not supposed to know what they mean," Jabo said. "They're God words. Only God, Jesus, and priests are supposed to know what they mean."

Jania (Yun-ya—girl) added, "The important thing is that these are sacred words, and Jesus likes to hear them. If that is what Jesus and the Blessed Virgin want to hear, then that's what we should sing."

"But they spoke Jewish," Kent said.

"What?" gasped Ziggy.

"I don't think Jesus, Mary, Joseph and the apostles ever spoke any Latin," Kent said. "They were Jewish and spoke Jewish. Everyone in the Bible spoke Jewish. Why aren't we singing these songs in Jewish?"

"Well, God likes Latin," Ziggy emphasized. "He made Jesus, the Blessed Virgin and everyone else in the Bible learn to speak Latin when they got to heaven, just like our parents had to learn English when they came to this country."

"Yea, but when our parents talk to each other, they talk in Polish," Jania said. "Even though Jesus and the Blessed Virgin are in heaven, I bet when they get together—just the two of them—they talk in Jewish……………………………………………………What is a virgin?"

ꕥꕥꕥ

The next morning, Jania, Kazik, Kent, Jabo, Pooza and I were sitting on the steps in front of the church waiting for class to begin. An older lady, walking on the sidewalk, passed by us for the third time that morning. Her eyes were swollen. She was crying. Clasping her hands together at throat level, she went to the rectory and knocked, but no one answered. She walked past us again and disappeared up the street.

Kent said, "This afternoon, we're going to confession. I'm going to have to confess saying the 'F' word in church."

"You said the 'F' word in church?" Pooza said rhetorically in amazement.

"Well, in the meeting room underneath the church. But that's pretty bad also, isn't it? If Father asks about it, I might have to tell him that I said the 'F' word at the same time that other guys in the class were saying it." Kazik, Jabo and Pooza twisted their bodies in Kent's direction, their eyes were glaring.

I jumped up and sat between Pooza and Kent. I put my arm around Kent and said, "I do not think the 'F' word underneath the church counts as a sin. What do you guys think?"

All of the other guys and Jania shook their heads and exclaimed, "Oh no, no way."

"Perhaps you should confess just the other sins on your list," I said.

"But I don't have any other sins."

"A whole week has passed, and you do not have any sins to confess?" I gasped. "Then you should tell Father that you do not have any sins this week. You may still take Holy Communion even if you have not gone to confession, if you do not carry the stain of sin."

"But Father expects us all to go to confession," Kent lamented. "How do I go to confession if I don't have any sins?"

"OK, then at confession, say that you forgot to say your evening prayers three times and that you disobeyed your mother … oh … say once."

"I can't say that," Kent objected. "I never miss my prayers. Those things did not happen."

"But those are the types of sins the priest expects to hear. Your life will be a lot easier if you just tell him want he wants to hear. You tell him those sins, and he will tell you to say three 'Our Fathers' and three 'Hail Marys' to the Blessed Virgin, and that will be the end of it."

"I can't lie in the confessional of all places."

"Have you killed anyone lately? Have you stolen?"

"No."

"Have you coveted your neighbor's wife?"

"No. I don't know?"

"God knows that you have been a good kid. God understands the jam that you are in with Father expecting you to go to confession. Under these circumstances, God would not think that you are lying. Nobody is suggesting that you lie. Instead, you are … you are … you are …" My eyes appealed for help among the other kids sitting on the steps.

Jania took the ball and said, "You are making a practice confession."

I pointed to her and clicked my fingers, "It is a practice confession."

Jania elaborated, "Remember three years ago when we prepared for our first Holy Communion? We practiced making a confession using example sins."

"A practice confession," Kent murmured.

Ziggy joined us on the steps as the distraught lady passed us for the fourth time. When she came to the sidewalk's location closest to the churchyard's shrine to the Blessed Virgin, she genuflected and sobbed as she made the sign of the cross three times. Ziggy whispered, "Do you know what that lady's problem is? She has two red bumps on her forehead. She thinks the devil is making her grow horns."

The priest emerged from the rectory and walked towards the growing gathering of students. When the lady on the sidewalk saw the priest, she tried to run to him, but she could manage only an enfeebled jog. When the priest caught sight of the lady, he instantaneously looked up at us on the steps. His facial expression turned to desperation as he quickened his pace to a speed walk. He passed us and intercepted the lady about fifty feet from us. His first actions were to turn the lady around and to start her moving away from us. The priest looked back at us, giving me the impression that he did not want us to observe the event.

๛๛๛

On Friday morning the students arrived to class to learn that Hania had been in a terrible car accident that morning and had died. A din hummed in my ears. A burning sensation drove through the back of my head as I labored to breath. Tremors in my legs dropped me into the folding chair I had been standing beside. Wailing and sobbing spread through the room. Kent stared in shock. With his hands clutching the front of his tee-shirt and arms fully extended downward, Kent was stretching the fabric. He attempted to speak, but no words came. He eventually was able to utter but one syllable, "Why!?"

Sister Theresa tearfully shook her head, swallowed and softly said, "Hania is with God now."

"No, No, No!" Kent cried. "I don't want her to be with God; I want her here." I had suspected that Kent was sweet on Hania. The memory of Hania talking with me a few days ago forced itself into my thoughts. I had joked with her that she would marry Pooza. The crushing reality that Hania would never marry anyone ripped my heart.

"Sister, you're going to have to explain this to me," Kent demanded. "Every week for years, I've come to catechism. You told us the first day that God loves us, that He cares for us. You told us that God is all-knowing and all-powerful—that He could do anything. You told us that everything that happens is by God's will. Now, I want you to explain to me why everything has gone so totally wrong."

Sister Theresa clutched the crucifix on her rosary. She was young and inexperienced and had no idea that an assignment to teach religious instruction to ten-year-olds would require her to face the most fundamental issues of her faith. "Yes, everything that happens is God's will. But we cannot expect to understand the plan He has for us."

"Bullshit! Those words aren't good enough now. If God's plan is for the purpose of doing good, then He's going to have to explain why Hania's death was necessary."

Catechism was cancelled for the remainder of the day. Everyone, except for Kent and me, lived close to the church in the hamlet along the river. Kent lived in the main part of Vandergrift, just over the hill about a quarter-mile away. I lived in Vandergrift heights, about a mile and a half away. When facing the ridge from the church, my house was to the left and mostly straight up through the woods that stretched along the steep slope of the ridge. Someone's folks would have given me a ride, but I did not feel like getting home soon and having to talk to anyone.

Three quarters of the way up the ridge I came to one of my favorite resting spots. I sat on the horizontal trunk of an uprooted tree, smooth by the absence of bark that had dissipated over time. I watched a cloud lose a strand of itself as it drifted easterly. "Why have you never talked to me?" I asked God. "In the Old Testament you talked like an old magpie to everyone and his brother. But you will not speak to me or anyone I know. This is like that stupid, stupid movie about that guy with a dog who talks. The dog blabs his chops off to his master. But if anyone else shows up, the dog clams up. People think the master is crazy because he claims his dog can talk. If you want to have a relationship, you are going to have to communicate with me. So far, it seems like I have been doing all of the talking. So, what is the big mystery? Why are you just sitting up there like a big stupe?" I watched a miniature-looking coal train in the valley straining to move upstream along the Kiskiminetas River. "How about making that train fly or turning the principal at Wilson School into a pillar of salt? That is a favorite of yours, is it not? You used to do that sort of thing all the time. I think you used to talk to people and do miracles because you wanted them to know that you were God and that you were big and bad and ready to kick their asses if they pissed you off. Well, I am sorry to inform you that you have a serious credibility problem right now. How is this for a deal? You bring Hania back to life, and I will do everything you tell me to do, forever. In fact, I bet that everyone in the catechism class would follow you forever. I know you can do it because you are omnipotent." I sat silently waiting for a sign. None appeared. "And I do not want to hear any of that 'doubting Thomas' bull. I thought it was so profound when I first heard the idea, blessed art thou who believeth without seeing. But now I think the idea is stupid. Suppose I were to tell the kids at Wilson School that unicorns really do exist, but to see one a person must first totally believe that unicorns exist, and if a person does not see any unicorns—it is because he just did not believe hard enough. If I told the kids that idea, they would send my underwear up the flagpole just to show their contempt for my stupidity. Everyone agrees that the lady who believes she is growing horns is mistaken. She really believes that she is growing horns. Maybe we are all like that lady, caught up in a colossal hoax. At least she has some red marks on her forehead. You have not given me any proof. The only difference between that lady believing she is growing horns and my believing you exist is that everyone says she is crazy and that everyone I know claims that you exist. And that is just not good enough anymore." I looked up at the darkening clouds. "I am sorry to rush you, God, but it looks like it is going to rain."

That was the day Hania died,………………………………….and so did god.

Chapter IV

A week before Labor Day, a new neighbor moved in across the street. I went over to introduce myself and to offer my services, for a fee. But first I surveyed as much of the property that I could see from the walkway and porch for potential jobs. I wielded the brass knocker. The lady, Mrs. Albemarle, told me that she did not have anything for me to do. Partially because I had nothing else to do and partially because the lady looked sort of poor, I offered to pullout the weeds from between the bricks in her walkways for ten cents. I ridiculously low balled the price because I liked to show some goodwill towards a potential, new client. Mrs. Albemarle engaged me. I went back to my house and returned to the job with a bucket, putty knife, pair of pliers and a pair of cloth work gloves that my dad had brought from the foundry where he works. For some of the weeds, I used pliers to clasp the weeds as closely as possible to the roots to facilitate extraction of as much root as possible. Using pliers and a putty knife made the job longer, but I had a high degree of professional pride in my weed pulling. An hour into the job, a little girl came from the house with a glass of lemonade for me.

"Thanks a lot," I said. "And thank your mum for me."

"OK, but mother did not make the lemonade. I thought you would be thirsty, so I made some." The girl sat on the grass with her legs crossed.

"This is good lemonade, good and tart, pretty good for a girl so little. How old are you?"

"Eight." She was small for an eight-year-old.

"My name is Daniel."

"Oooh, I like your name. How do you spell it?"

"D-A-N-I-E-L, the same as DAN-yil, but mine is pronounced dun-yell. What is your name?"

"Mary Jane."

"Oooh, I like that name," I echoed her. "Well, Mary Jane, where was home before now?"

"Home was in Frostburg, Maryland. But we spent this summer in Charlottesville, Virginia. That is where Thomas Jefferson's home is."

"No kidding, the Monticello? That is where it is? In Charlottesville, Virginia?" I was impressed by the experience of someone so small.

"Yea, Mr. Jefferson had a big house and a bunch of tiny little houses for his Negro slaves. Did you know that he had slaves?"

"No, I did not know that any president owned slaves." I was skeptical about Mary Jane's claim. However, Lincoln freed the Negroes, and he was the sixteenth president. As the third president, Jefferson lived many years before the slaves were freed. Jefferson lived in the South. Maybe she was telling the truth. I made a mental note to look up Mary Jane's claim in the encyclopedia next time I went to the library. "Do you have any brothers and sisters?" Mary Jane shook her head no. "Do you know anyone in Vandergrift?" She shook her head a sad no. "Then, what do you do all day?"

"I read *Cultures of the World* magazines. Some of them have maps folded inside. I spend a lot of time looking at the maps and daydreaming about what places would be like. Every time we visit my grandfather, he lets me borrow a stack of his old magazines."

"What grade are you in?" I asked.

"Third grade."

"And you read *Cultures of the World*? I do not believe it."

"Yes, I do. OK, I always carry a dictionary with me and have to look up a lot of the words. Sometimes, I have to look up the words that describe the word that I looked up. But I do read the magazines and look at the maps."

"OK, then what is the country directly southwest of Germany?" I quizzed her.

"That is easy, France," Mary Jane replied without hesitation.

"Hey, that is pretty good. I know what it is like to read maps and daydream. I do that too."

I finished pulling and digging out the weeds. Mrs. Albemarle was impressed. "I have another job you can do for me. I see that you've met Mary Jane. She doesn't know anyone in this town. I'll pay you a penny each day to walk her to school and back. That's a nickel for the week."

What a deal. I thought, {*A nickel added to the thirty cents I get for milk money would increase my weekly school earnings by … 16.6 percent, just to do what I normally do anyway; walk to school.*}

❧❧❧

While walking to school on the second day, Mary Jane and I saw a duck jump from the curb on our side of the street and waddle to the center. It had the dull brown colors of a female. She was soon followed by a dozen small ducklings. The ensemble waddled to the curb on the other side of the street. The mother hopped the curb and waited for the ducklings to follow. The ducklings made repeated attempts to jump the curb, but kept falling back in failure. The quarry-stone blocks of the curb were unusually tall, having been pushed up by ages of frost heaves. The curb blocks looked like the long, lower front teeth of a very old person. A coal truck crested the hill. The driver shifted into second gear to slow the descent. The ducklings frantically continued attempting to hurdle the curb. I went into the street to draw the attention of the driver and to flag him to a stop, if physically possible. Mary Jane ran across the street to shoo the ducklings over the curb.

"Get out of the street!" I yelled to her.

"Should I try to pick them up?!" Mary Jane hollered back.

"No, you will only make them scatter. Then we will really have a mess." The truck's horn sounded, and its breaks started to screech. "Get off the street!"

"What can we do?!" Mary Jane shouted.

"I don't know. Get out of the street!" I turned to run towards Mary Jane to grab her and pull her to safety when I saw that she had laid her aluminum lunchbox flat on the street, abutting the curb. Extending from the lunchbox, she set a stack of two books from her book bag. She shooed the ducklings towards the stairway she had constructed. The truck's horn blew. I threw my left arm around Mary Jane's waist and my right arm around her chest and hoisted her over the curb. We watched as the ducklings scampered in quick succession up Mary Jane's books and lunchbox and over the curb. The truck driver barked obscenities at us as he drove by.

I stared at the stairway, marveling at its ingenuity. I stepped off the curb, leaned over and retrieved Mary Jane's books and lunchbox. I handed the lunchbox to her. I returned the books to her book bag and slung the strap of the bag over my shoulder.

"You are carrying my books? So, you are not mad with me?"

"Oh, I am angry alright. I bet your mum would not pay me if I let you get crushed by a coal truck."

๛๛๛

The next morning, Angelin and Joanie walked to school with Mary Jane and me. Angelin was not keen on the idea of walking to school with a third grader. But she knew there was no dissuading me when I was engaged in paid employment. Mary Jane talked about a feature in *Cultures of the World* on the Lapp people and the land of reindeer and the midnight sun. The story was fascinating. She told us that the Lapps are nomadic and do not recognize national boundaries. She pulled a folded map from her book bag and pointed to northern Sweden, Finland and Russian Soviet Union.

"I don't see *Lapland* written anywhere," Angelin said sassingly.

"This is a political map, and Lapland is not a country," Mary Jane explained. "The Lapps are nomadic, moving their reindeer often while looking for the sparse vegetation. They cross national boundaries without even knowing it. The Lapp people are short and have stubby, fat fingers to preserve heat and to avoid frostbite."

∾∾∾

After three weeks of school, I felt crummy about continuing to collect nickels from Mary Jane's mum. Opportunities to make money abounded for me. I did not have to squeeze nickels from a poor lady. However, the walk to school routine did not change. Joanie picked up Angelin. They picked up me, and the three of us picked up Mary Jane.

∾∾∾

Joanie invited me to her house to play Monopoly. I told her that Monopoly was not much of a game with only three players. I suggested she invite Mary Jane as a fourth player.

"But Angelin doesn't like Mary Jane," Joanie cautioned.

"I am not sure how Angelin feels about Mary Jane," I said. "It is hard to say when Angelin really does not like something or when she is just being her normal cranky self. Look, Mary Jane has no brother or sister, nor does she have any friends other than us. She is clever, and I like her."

On the way to Joanie's house, I stopped to pick up Mary Jane. When Mary Jane and I arrived at Joanie's house, we found her dancing with her mother. They danced that very energetic way that soldier boys do in the movies. Joanie's mother called it swing dancing. They invited me to join them. But I refused to engage in such a sissy activity. Undeterred, both ran to me and jerked me out of the chair in which I had been sitting. They taught me the footing that included a rock step. We practiced the underarm turn. I danced with Joanie, then with Mary Jane, and then back with Joanie. When Angelin arrived, she refused to try to dance, which surprised me because I thought that girls were predisposed to know how to, and wanted to, dance. Angelin was just being contrary and was waiting for us to beg her to join us. Joanie, Mary Jane and I swarmed her and dragged her to the center of the parlor. Angelin acted as if she were terrifically bored. But, just like I, she loved it. The triplets were a tag team, sharing time dancing with me. Each of them got breaks, but I did not. It was quite a workout. Joanie persuaded her mother to show us the steps to the rhumba. The basic box, long-quick-quick / long-quick-quick, was easy enough. The girls giggled when Joanie's mother had me hunch my hips to attempt performance of the Cuban walk. I was intrigued by the technique to achieve the underarm turn in the rhumba. The boy signals the start of the turn by using his left hand to raise the girl's right hand. While raising the arm, the boy backs up on his right foot, creating separation from the girl so that she can start the inward turn. The girl uses two sets of beats to complete a 270 degree turn to her right. The boy slides a quarter-turn to his left to meet the girl head on when she has completed the gyration. I came to enjoy ballroom dancing in Joanie's parlor during many Saturdays when the weather was nasty. I became good at it. I certainly got enough practice, having to satisfy the tag team of Joanie, Mary Jane and Angelin.

Chapter V

I went over to Joanie's house to see the boil that had grown in her left armpit. The boil was so painful that she could not comfortably dangle her arm. Joanie had to hold her arm arcing away from her body, like a muscleman. Joanie looked scared. Her father used a set of pliers to hold a double-edged razorblade. He sterilized the razorblade in the flame from a burner on the natural gas stove. Joanie showed me the boil by raising her left arm straight up and resting the forearm atop her head. Wew, the boil was a beaut. It was hot and white in the center.

"I'm scared, Daniel," Joanie whimpered as she stared at the razorblade. "Isn't there some other way?"

"I would do it another way. I would have someone shove a book deeply underneath the boil. Then I would take another book and slam it right down onto the boil. In a split second, the core is shot to the moon."

"I don't think so."

"Then I would not do anything," I said. "No one ever died from a boil. Sometime, when you least expect it, you will accidentally bump it. The pussy core would pop out. And just like that, the problem is resolved without even being traumatized by it." Joanie's dad wrapped half of the razorblade with adhesive tape. As he walked towards us, Joanie's grip on my arm tightened. I could feel her terror traveling from her hand into my arm. In a panic, I cried, "Wait!"

"What, Daniel?" Joanie's dad sighed impatiently.

"Ah … ah … Let Joanie do it."

"Me?" Joanie screeched.

"It is a lot less frightening if the blade is handled by you," I explained. "You decide when to cut, how much to cut and when to take a break. With the blade in your own fingers, it hurts less because you know that the pain cannot get so bad that you cannot stand it. If someone else does the cutting, you do not know how much it will hurt and when the hurt will start and stop. And that fear of the unknown hurts more and earlier than the actual cutting."

"I'll try it. Give me the razorblade." We followed Joanie into the bathroom. She leaned against the sink to get close to the mirror and to calm her tremors. She wrapped her left arm over the top of her head, revealing the abscess. Joanie slowly moved the razorblade towards her armpit. Her hand quivered. Sweat beads formed on her forehead and upper lip. A sweat drop inched down the inner side of her upper arm.

"Wait," I said with a poorly faked, calm voice. I ran back into the kitchen and fetched the stool used to reach the upper shelves. I placed the stool atop the bathroom sink and held onto the stool to give it stability. "Rest your elbow on the stool. Your hand will not shake as much."

Joanie touched the boil with the blade, but did not cut into it. She swallowed, closed her eyes and reopened them. She slowly drew the blade along the head of the boil, making a small slit. Joanie rested her hand on the stool and asked, "How 'm I doin'?"

I touched the small of Joanie's back with the palm of my left hand. Her blouse was soaked. "You are doing great, kid." I gave her a moment to rest her nerve. I then said, "Using the blade closest to the tape, work the edge into the skin groove you made. Then slide the blade through the groove, pressing a little harder this time."

Joanie nodded slightly while shutting her eyes slightly. She puffed her upper lip and blew air from it. She inserted the blade into the slit and again drew the blade through it. Suddenly, she jerked away the hand with the blade held in its fingers. She threw her head back while wincing her face and inhaling a burst of air through her teeth. Joanie's hand quivered as she rested it on the stool. Her elbow sagged to her eyebrows as she sobbed, "I can't do this any more."

"Wait," I said as I clutched her arm and slid the crook of Joanie's elbow back to the top of her head. I watched her wound as a red outline rolled from one end of the slit to the other. "I do not think that you have to cut anymore."

Joanie's eyes shot to the image of the boil in the mirror. "But it's still there."

"From here, you can squeeze it out," I said. "Put your thumb on one side of the boil and your fingers on the other side. Push hard into your armpit to try to get behind the boil." As Joanie surrounded the boil, the head became whiter from the increased pressure. "Now, keep trying to get behind the boil and squeeze."

"It hurts, Daniel."

"Keep squeezing…Keep squeezing."

"It hurts. I don't think …" Pop, the core squirted out like a newborn bunny and landed on Joanie's wrist. "Oooh, yuk," Joanie cried as if she had been puked on by an alien monster.

"Do not move," I said as I plunged a hand into my pocket to retrieve my pocketknife. I opened the largest blade and moved it towards Joanie's wrist, saying "Do not move. I will scrape the core off of you." The core looked rubbery, like the embryo in a chicken egg that had remained in the nest too long. "You did it," I cheered. Joanie's head slumped forward in exhausted relief. I leaned forward and rested my forehead against hers. Raising her eyes to flow into mine, she asked, "That's it?"

"That is it."

"That's it?"

"That is it. The boil will ooze a little bit today. But you do not have to touch it again."

"Could we sit down?" Joanie commanded more that asked. I followed her into the kitchen where she passed up the hard chairs around the kitchen table and, instead, continued into the parlor. She flopped onto the couch. I sat beside her. "It feels so good to just sit here and to have that over with," Joanie said.

Joanie's older brother, Ralphy, entered the parlor, turned on the television and sat on the floor. It took a couple of minutes for the vacuum tubes to warm up before a faint picture appeared. The television was housed in a large console and had a nine-inch diagonally measured screen. Joanie's family had the only television in the neighborhood. Ralphy's favorite show, *Glory Squad*, was about to start. "Isn't it the neatest show?" Ralphy's question was probably directed to me.

"I saw the show a few times at my cousin's house," I replied. "It bored me after the fourth episode." Ralphy looked surprised and frowned because I did not share his enthusiasm. I explained, "All of the shows were the same. The American soldiers come to a French village where they discover German soldiers holed up in a shop with a sign painted on it saying 'Bureau Tabac'. Both sides shoot a million shots, but no one gets hit. Then an American chucks a hand grenade—that looks like a small grayish-green pineapple—through the window of the Bureau Tabac, killing a couple dozen Germans. The strange thing is … none of the Germans ever get wounded. You never see anyone crawling around wounded and crying in pain. The Germans are either alive or dead and nothing in between. When the Americans go into the Bureau Tabac, they do not see any blood or guts or body parts strewn about, as you would expect from an explosion. Instead, the Germans are just lying around neatly as if they had exhausted themselves at recess and were now taking a nap. It is different, though, when the Germans find the Americans holed up in the Bureau Tabac. The Germans chuck in a grenade that is on a stick that looks like a tom-tom drumstick. I guess the Germans can chuck a grenade farther by using the stick for leverage. Back when an American chucks a hand grenade, he waits a couple of seconds after he pulls the safety pin to shorten the time left on the explosion timer. As soon as the American hand grenade clears the window, it explodes. The Krauts do not have a chance. But when the Germans toss a grenade at the Americans in the Bureau Tabac, the Americans get to look at it for a couple of minutes and look for a place to hide so they would not get blown up when it explodes. Sometimes the Americans lay a mattress on the grenade. I think the Americans must have carried mattresses with them to use when grenades were chucked their way. I also think that the Germans might have won the war if the timers on their grenades were not set so long. I do not know why the American army made its soldiers lug those heavy rifles everywhere. It would have made more sense to forget about the rifles and to issue the soldiers newspaper boy bags chocked full of hand grenades. Then when the Americans ran into the Germans, the Americans could duck and start flinging grenades in all directions until all of the Germans run away."

Agape, Ralphy countered, "The Americans have to carry rifles, stupe. They need rifles so that the officers can say 'fix bayonets' because they like saying 'fix bayonets'… Isn't there anything about the show you like?"

I thought about it and responded, "I like the German uniforms, especially for the officers. They are really spiffy. The American uniforms look like they came from the Derailment Thrift Store. I also like how the Germans click their heels when saluting. I have tried to click my heels, but I cannot match the reverberation heard like when a German soldier does it. They must put cleats on the sides of their heels." Ralphy sprang to his feet. He clicked his heels and did the "Heil Hitler" salute. "See, you cannot do it either," I chuckled. Annoyed by my chiding, Ralphy clicked his heels and saluted again, and again … and again …

Joanie elbowed me in the ribs and said, "I just got a new issue of *Cultures of the World.* The feature is on the orangoutangs of Borneo. Want to read it?"

"Wow, are you kidding? Yea!"

Joanie stood up, and I followed her to the entrance to the kitchen. Joanie asked her folks if she and I could go up to her bedroom to read *Cultures of the World.* Her dad scoffed, "You can't take a boy up to your bedroom."

Joanie's mom, who taught me how to dance, winced while glancing at her husband through the corners of her eyes. She pushed a hand wave towards us and nodded her consent.

"Thanks," Joanie said. As she turned, Joanie grabbed my right arm and spun me around. I followed her lead out of the kitchen and through the parlor towards the stairway at the front door. Apparently, Joanie construed parental ambiguities in the light most favorable to her. We scampered up the stairs to her room. "Who reads?" Joanie asked.

"It is the boil-busting-girl's choice."

"So, you're gonna make the whole day a special day for me?" Joanie asked. "OK then, you read." Joanie puffed up a pillow at the head of the bed and sat her back against it. She pulled another pillow across her lap and rested her arms on it. At the foot of the bed, I sat on my right leg and let my left leg dangle over the edge to the floor. During the first few minutes of the reading, Joanie slowly sunk from her erect sitting position. Within ten minutes, she was asleep. I twisted my body and clasped the blanket setting atop the cedar chest at the foot of the bed. I spread the blanket over the boil-busting-girl.

✥✥✥

"What are those bumps on your chest?" a smirking Joanie asked of Angelin while I was gone from the parlor. It was the spring of Joanie's year in fifth grade and Angelin's sixth.

"They're two seething boils that just happened to have festered in the same spot on both sides of my chest," Angelin quipped. The Italian girls seemed to develop breasts at a younger age than all of the other girls.

Chapter VI

"Oooh, oooh, oooh," Joanie, Mary Jane and I moaned in unison, disgusted by the gossip Angelin had heard during her first week at Vandergrift Junior High School. Angelin had just started seventh grade. Joanie and I were in sixth, and Mary Jane was in fourth.

"And then the man pushes …"

"Oooh, stop," Joanie pleaded. "You're gonna make me vomit."

"That is the most ridiculous story I have ever heard," I said. "I cannot believe you actually repeated it to us."

"The eighth-grade girls in my gym class swear that that's how babies are made," Angelin insisted.

"Well, if it is true, then that explains why adults are so secretive and mysterious when it comes to the subject of sex," I said. "It also explains why jerky, older guys snicker when they see a girl wearing a tight sweater in the movies. And this is the best reason I have heard to prove that God does not exist."

"Good grief, Daniel," an exasperated Joanie moaned. "How is this proof that God does not exist?"

"If you were omniscient and omnipotent, is this system the best you could come up with? I mean, if you had a choice between the Holy Ghost sprinkling baby dust on all of the good wives as they slept or a man doing to a woman what you just described, which would you choose? Why choose the most disgusting thing you could possibly think of? It does not appear as if there was any planning involved in this system."

"I guess that's why Mary was a virgin," Angelin said sarcastically. "After all, you wouldn't want that happening to the mother of Christ."

I said, "I do not think that I will ever get married. But if I do get married, I think I will follow the Saint Joseph model." I watched a woman on the sidewalk across the street push a stroller with a toddler in it. "OK, that woman over there has a baby. You are telling me that since she has that baby, then that woman right there must have taken off her clothes, and her husband also took his clothes off, and she let this naked guy lie on top of her and…? I do not believe it."

"That happened to her and also to everyone who has had children," Angelin proclaimed. We sat silently in contemplation. The more we thought, the wider our eyes grew. I glanced at Joanie, Joanie glanced at Mary Jane, Mary Jane glanced at Angelin.

"Everyone?!" Joanie gasped. "No, nah-ah, no, no."

"Oh no, no, no," I exclaimed. "My folks do not kiss. They do not hug. They never touch each other. And you expect me to believe that my mum and dad … No. This is a ridiculous idea. It never happened."

"Your mom and dad sleep in the same bed, don't they?" Angelin queried. "That's when it happens."

Without having yet absorbed the full shock of the moment, I blurted out, "But I have a brother and three sisters. Are you telling me that my parents did that foul thing five times?"

"Yea."

"But why?" I demanded. "The newsreel at the movies talked about a global overpopulation problem, billions and billions of people. Why are all of these people getting together, getting naked and doing this thing? After all, would you do it, or you, or you?"

"Oooh, yuck, no way!" Joanie cried as she shivered and wiped away imaginary yuckies from her dress.

"Exactly the point," I continued. "Why are billions of people doing this gross thing over and over again?"

"Because God commands it," Joanie replied.

"Where does God command such queer behavior?"

"Be fruitful and multiply," Angelin said.

"Yea, be fruitful and multiply. Didn't you ever hear that, Daniel?" Joanie asked.

I leaned forward and dumped my head into my hands. "So, you are telling me that those words do not command us to grow fruit trees?" Angelin and Joan burst out laughing. Mary Jane remained silent, but listened intently. Her sparse religious education restricted her ability to participate in the discussion. I said, "I thought I was clever to interpret the fruitful-and-multiply command as meaning that people must be productive. Farmers should grow crops. Iron workers should make lots of iron. Teachers should do a good job teaching kids. Why did God say it that way? Why not just say 'make babies'?"

Mary Jane asked, "What is the connection between doing this sex thing and being married?"

"I guess you would have to say that they are linked … when it comes to making a baby," I replied.

"No, Daniel," Angelin countered. "An unmarried man can make a baby, and an unmarried woman can get pregnant."

"Really?" I said. "I have never seen a lady with a child who was not also married."

"Well, it happens," Angelin said. "Why do you ask, Mary Jane?"

Mary Jane was uncharacteristically quiet and sullen. She said, "Some things about my daddy do not make sense. My mother says that she and my daddy were married just before he had to leave for the army and that he died a hero during the war. But there are no pictures of him, no wedding pictures, no wedding dress, no letters, no grand-parents, no cousins. Each of you has a father and a mother who sleep together. My mother has had many boyfriends, and they all have slept in her bed. Have you ever seen anything like that?"

Angelin and Joanie glanced at each other.

ৡৡৡ

Angelin and I left Joanie's house and escorted Mary Jane to her house. I normally would have walked across the street to my house, but I walked Angelin to her house, instead, because I wanted to talk to her. "What was Mary Jane talking about?" I asked.

"Daniel, you are so smart about some things. But when it comes to people things, you are stone stupid." Angelin's words were a sting-ing insult but were true. She said, "Mary Jane is a bastard."

"Why are you calling her a bad name?"

"Do you know the meaning of the word *bastard*?" Angelin asked.

"Yea, sure. A bastard is … a jerk."

"And what is the real meaning of the word, bastard ?"

"Are you saying that the word has a meaning other than a way to badmouth someone? Do you mean a meaning that you could find in a dictionary?" I asked.

"I don't know if the word is in the dictionary, but it might be."

"I will see you later," I said as I turned around and ran towards my house. I drew the dictionary from the bookshelf in the family room and thumbed through to the word bastard. I was amazed to discover that the word was indeed in the dictionary. I ran back to Angelin's house. I went to the back door, and Angelin let me into the kitchen. She offered, and I accepted, a glass of cold, sugared tea from a pitcher.

"What are you frowning about?" Angelin asked.

I shook my head and sighed. "Some people think that I am smart. My Aunt Wanda points to me and says, 'There's a smart boy.'" I smirked as I coughed a breath out of my nose. "I did not think that I knew everything in the world, especially about sciences and far away places. But I thought I had my world figured out. Now I am finding that there are big piles of stuff all around me that I do not know. I need to find out what is really happening around me. And I want to start right now." I looked at Angelin and said, "I need to see what a girl's private parts look like."

"And I'm the girl you want to look at? No way, Daniel. You're crazy."

"Why not?"

"Because … because it's not decent."

"Not decent by whose rules?" I retorted. "Our parents? Don't we already know that we have to start making our own rules? Besides, I am willing to trade you something you very much want."

"What?"

"I will let you see me." I could tell by her reaction that she was as curious as I. Her failure to quickly reject the offer made me believe that she would agree. "The woods would be the safest place to do it."

"That takes too long," Angelin objected. "Besides, the sight of you and me entering the woods looks suspicious. Someday, a prankster is gonna follow us. No, we will do it here, up in my bedroom." My eyes and ears perked up to try to detect the presence of anyone else in the house. Angelin said, "My grandma is visiting her mother at the nursing home. She won't be back for an hour and a half."

When we entered her bedroom, Angelin said, "You first." I did not need to unbutton my pants because I had no ass and no hips. With a sense of guilt like a thief at night, I slowly dropped my pants, followed by my underpants.

With an expression of surprise Angelin under-exclaimed, "Oh." She leaned forward to get a closer look. She extended her index finger in a manner that suggested she was about to touch me. I reflexively shuffled backwards, awkwardly because my pants were binding me at the knees.

"Oh what?" I asked.

"Is that all there is? That is the reason I cannot be a doctor, or train engineer or be in the army?"

"What more do I need to simply pee? It works well for me … OK, now it is your turn," I said as I pulled up my pants and underpants together. Angelin used her thumb to pry the elastic waistband four inches away from her belly. She looked down as if she were inspecting her private parts to make sure nothing had changed from earlier that day. She swiftly pulled down her bloomers and stared at the ceiling. I looked intently and gasped, "Holy-moly. Are you sure your private parts are normal for a girl? Maybe you should have a doctor examine you. It looks like you have two abscessed tumors."

Angelin slapped me on the head and huffed, "Believe me, I saw dozens of girls in the shower room after gym class on Thursday. They all look like this."

We did not want to press any further our chances of not being detected. So, Angelin pulled up her bloomers, and we went to sit on the swing on the front porch. I said, "The sex thing does not sound like something I would want to do, even if I were married. So, why have Mary Jane's mother and her boyfriends done it when they were not married and were not being commanded by God to be fruitful and to multiply? Also, I've heard some married people say that they had, say, six kids, but they only wanted three. But if they did not want to do a disgusting thing in the first place and also did not want to have anymore kids after three, then why bother to do the disgusting sex thing anyway?"

"It's because God expects them to continue having more children," Angelin replied.

"But most of the people of the world are not Christian, and yet, they are begetting overpopulation throughout the world"

"I bet that other religions also have the be-fruitful-and-multiply rule," Angelin said.

"But still, it seems like there's too much zeal involved in having babies. Many people are told to lose weight, or they will have heart attacks, but they continue to gorge on potatoes fried in lard. Your grandfather continues to smoke, even though the cigarettes have given him emphysema. So, I do not think that mere compliance with some rule to do a disgusting thing caused the begetting of billions of people.

ﭢﭢﭢ

Angelin's grandfather had just had all of his teeth surgically extracted. He was in bed and in extreme pain. An unusually early frost threatened his two fig trees. The winters are harsh in the Appalachian foothills, northeast of Pittsburgh. Yet, many of the Italian immigrants in the area successfully cultivated small fig trees. To keep them from freezing, the branches had to be buried each fall and exhumed each spring. Angelin, Mary Jane and I performed the fall preparation for Angelin's grandfather. One by one, I bent the branches to the ground. The girls stood on the branches as I pounded two-foot long staples into the ground to hold down the branches. We retrieved old discarded rugs from the garage. The rugs were laid atop the bent branches, with bricks anchoring the edges. Finally, we piled mounds of leaves, grass clippings and garden debris on top the rugs to provide insulation. When the trees are uncovered in spring, forked sticks would be pried under the branches to coax them to grow skyward again.

Chapter VII

After hundreds of odd jobs and money making schemes during the past four years, I had accumulated three hundred dollars in savings. Responding to an advertisement in the business section of a Pittsburgh newspaper, I submitted an application to a stockbrokerage to open an account. I lied about my age. I claimed that I was thirty years old. I had to wait for my dad's payday to accompany him to the bank. After he deposited his paycheck, my dad gave the clerk permission to issue a cashier's check for three hundred dollars, drawn from my savings account and made payable to the brokerage firm. After the brokerage firm cashed the check, the thirty-year-old Daniel instructed the brokerage by letter to purchase a hundred shares of stock in a company that made plumbing supplies. I chose plumbing supplies because I presumed that a customer will buy plumbing supplies even if he was hard up for dough because he cannot let his pipes leak or, worse yet, his toilet. I figured that a plumbing company has to give high dividends because it is not jazzy, like a baseball team, or a movie company, or a company that makes perfume. People might want to own stock in those companies just because they are cool, regardless of the payoff to the stockholders. I thought I might use the same reasoning in choosing a career someday. I figured that the least probability for successful careers, money wise, would be in sports, movies, music and the arts. If a job looks like it is too much fun, then people probably would not want to pay you for doing it. Or, if the job looks enjoyable, then too many people will bust their butts trying to get it. For every professional sports job available, I bet there are thousands and thousands of want-to-be's who do not have a prayer of landing the job, but who are wasting their time and money preparing for the illusive opportunity. If

I wanted someday to earn a lot of dough, I thought I should pick a career that had more openings than people who wanted that type of job. I thought I might consider being an accountant. It looked like it must be the most boring job imaginable. An employer would have to pay a ton of money for me to sit in an office and add numbers all day, day after day.

Soon after acquiring the stock, I discovered that I would receive the six dollar annual dividend in about a month and a half. I was astounded by the idea that I would soon receive a check for more money than I had ever received at any job.

ھ∕ھ∕ھ∕

Mary Jane asked me to accompany her on an errand across town to deliver something at the house of the brother of her mother's boyfriend. I declined, saying that I had to get started on a large leaf-raking job for old Mrs. Szczpinovska. Joanie, looking desperate, pleaded with me to reconsider. She said, "Spike's brother scares me. I would not ask you unless I really needed your help."

"No problem," I said. "I can rake this afternoon. But you will have to tell Joanie and Angelin that we cannot dance until four ah'clock, and all of you will have to live with my not having a bath after the raking."

"It is a deal," Mary Jane celebrated with gratitude seemingly too heartfelt for the mere favor granted.

"What is in the sack?" I asked, nodding at the satchel at Mary Jane's side hanging by a strap around her shoulder. She shrugged without replying. I took a step towards Mary Jane's side, but she flinched backwards. Realizing how ridiculous it was to expect me to walk with her to the other side of town without revealing the identity of the cargo, she flipped open the flap, signaling permission for me to inspect the contents. I saw two zinc jar lids. I placed a hand into the satchel and pulled out one of the two Mason jars with water in it. I looked at Mary Jane with a puzzled expression.

"It is moonshine," Mary Jane said.

I was surprised. Having never before seen moonshine, I would have expected it to have the caramel color of whiskey. I was also surprised that the substance still existed in modern days. Moonshine was a commodity of the Prohibition era during the Great Depression and the saga of Elliot Ness and the Untouchables. I gently tried to open the lid, but it was tight. I ceased the attempt because the lid might have had a vacuum seal that I did not want to breach. "Your mother's boyfriend makes moonshine?" I asked rhetorically.

Mary Jane sadly rolled her eyes.

When we arrived, Spike's brother sneered, "So you brought your boyfriend with you this time." Mary Jane blushed. Spike's brother was a jerk. I instinctively stretched myself to be as tall as I could and tried to look like a tough guy. He paid Mary Jane with a five dollar bill. He offered to dish out ice cream for us, but we said that we had to go. He gave each of us a candy bar, and we left. Walking home, Mary Jane acted giddy with relief. She ripped into her candy bar in celebration. I squirreled mine into my jacket pocket. It was a five cent bar. I estimated that I could get three, maybe four, cents for it during recess at school. As we crossed the arched, stone bridge over Beaver Run, Mary Jane retrieved the candy wrapper from her pocket and tossed it, presumably into the run. We detoured into a cemetery covered by huge oak trees. The footpath was calf deep in leaves. We frolicked and giggled as we kicked up the leaves. When we arrived at Mary Jane's house, I waved and said, "I will pick you up around four." I broke into a jog towards my house because I was keen on changing into my grubby, torn clothes and get to the job for Mrs. Szczpinovska. I could not have been in the house half a minute, when I heard a pounding at the back door. I did not bother to put a shirt back on and walked swiftly to answer the door. Mary Jane was panting, her visage panicky.

"It's gone! I can't find it!" Mary Jane blurted between gulps of air.

"What is gone?"

"The money, the five dollars, I can't find it!"

I extended my right arm towards the interior of the kitchen as an invitation for Mary Jane to enter. I took hold of her upper arm and led her to a chair at the kitchen table. Mary Jane clasped her arms around her waist and bent forward as if fighting off a debilitating cramp. "Oh my God," Mary Jane wailed, "I threw it away with that stupid candy wrapper." Even though the money was not mine, the thought of losing five dollars by such a careless act made me sick.

"Where did you throw it away?"

Mary Jane thought for a while and then cried, "Over the bridge!" That thought made me even sicker. "We gotta go back and find it, Daniel. You will go with me and help, won't you?"

"Look girl, I am the cheapest guy in the world. And if I thought there was a chance in hell of finding the money, I would be the first one there. But that run has thick brush along both banks for over a mile. Mary Jane, I am sorry. But there is absolutely no chance of finding the money." Mary Jane clasped her arms around her head and sobbed uncontrollably. I knelt on one knee, placed a hand on her shoulder and bowed my head to enable me to look up into her face. I said calmly, "Losing five bucks that way is bad. There is no question about it. But it is not the end of the world. After all, how bad can it be when you tell your mum … and Spike?" Mary Jane's lower lip quivered. She shut her eyes and tears streamed out the slits as she slowly shook her head. I was so gripped by her despair that I muttered to myself a thought that I had never before conceived, "It is only money." In a few days I was to receive six dollars in dividends for not having done anything, except for not having spent a dime of earnings for years. None of the candy, toys or clothes that one could buy ever seemed worth the price. Yet, I worked and saved fiendishly with the conviction that someday something will be so important that I would be willing to spend any amount to have it. I had also been driven by the notion that when the realization happened, I would not be denied because of a lack of money. I looked at Mary Jane's quivering lower lip, and I knew that that was the time and that was the contingency. I said, "I have five dollars you can have." Mary Jane kept sobbing. She must not have heard me. I pushed her right arm away from the side of her head to awaken her from the stupor. The palm of my hand wiped the tears from her left eye, and I continued to slide the hand around the side of her face and rested at the back of her head. "Hey listen, I said that I have five dollars you can have."

It took a moment for the words to sink into Mary Jane's cognition. "You have five dollars that you are willing to give me?"

"Yea, all of those jobs eventually add up to real money."

"But how can I take that much money from you?"

"Suppose the situation was reversed. Suppose you had jobs lined up for two weeks—mowing grass, pulling weeds, cleaning toilets, painting fences. But you are not going to get paid in money. Instead, the payoff for your work is that I would not have to suffer the anguish like the kind you are feeling now. Would you make the deal? Would you work two weekends and every evening after school for two weeks just to take away the pain from me similar to yours right now?"

"Yea, I would do it."

"Well, that is what I am doing. Forget about the middle step where people pay me money and I give the money to you. What it really is—I work two weeks, and your suffering stops. That sounds like a bargain…I will be right back." I went to my bedroom and stuck my arm under the bed to retrieve the cigar box from a sling dangling a few inches from underneath the bedsprings. The sling was constructed from dozens of interwoven pieces of twine the butcher had used to hold the paper wrappings around the family meat purchases. I went to the wall on the other side of the room and used a wire clothes hanger to fish the padlock key dangling on a long string behind the hot water radiator. Placing the cigar box atop the radiator, I opened and removed the padlock. I snatched the four, one-dollar bills lying on the top. On the bottom was a chaos of marbles, used batteries and coins. I scooped the marbles and batteries and stashed them in a makeshift pouch created from a stinky tee-shirt. I dumped the coins onto the bedspread and counted a dollar's worth. It was a close call, only seven cents to spare. I returned to the kitchen and presented the loot to Mary Jane.

Mary Jane frowned and said, "But Spike gave me a five dollar bill."

I shook my head as I said, "You are slipping over the edge, girl. Spike expects five dollars, and that is what he is going to get. He does not care what it looks like… Now, is there anything else with which we must deal?"

Mary Jane sighed and lamented, "Daniel, I do not have a job. How on earth will I ever be able to repay you?"

"Do not worry. I am never at a loss to think of schemes for making money. For example, my three-year job as the milk boy at school will end in a few months. I can suggest to the principal that you take over the job. You could start when you are in fifth grade, when I go to the junior high. There has never been a milk girl, but there is a first time for everything. You are small, but you are wiry and strong. I know you can do it."

"Do you really think that you can get me the job?"

"Oh yea, the principal is clueless. She is open to my suggestions. You can go with me on the milk run for a couple of weeks. Does your mother give you milk money?"

"Uh-huh," Mary Jane nodded.

"The milk run gets you free milk. So, you can pay me thirty cents each week." I looked at an imaginary calculation on the ceiling. "Dividing three into fifty, that is sixteen, nearly seventeen, weeks of stacking and hauling milk to pay off the five dollars. Is it worth it?"

"Are you kidding? I would deliver milk for twenty years to get me out of this jam. Besides, I really want to be the milk boy … or girl." Mary Jane looked down at the money she held in her hand. "Oh, Daniel …" She sprang from her seat, flung her arms around me and hugged me tightly. "You saved my life. You may not realize it, and it may not be a big deal to you. But you saved my life."

"Your mother is expecting you. You better get home and give her the money."

Chapter VIII

When I had started sixth grade, none of the girls in my grade sported breasts, except for chunky Darlene. I did not know whether she had actual breasts or just fat rolls strategically located. But as the year progressed, two by two, breasts popped out throughout the class like mushroom buttons. Joanie was in my class. However, she did not develop until junior high school. By the end of sixth grade, I experienced my own episodes involving puberty. Every day I could not wait to get home from school. I went straight to my bedroom to put on an old pajama bottom. I did not want to foul my jeans. My new and strange behavior did not go unnoticed. My mum unexpectedly entered my bedroom, catching me in the act. I was embarrassed as Mum touched me in the crotch, apparently checking for wetness. Mum told me that I was doing a disgusting and sinful thing. She told me that if I did not stop, I would become addicted. She said, "You'll end up like those dirty men on the street corners downtown. They stand there all day with their hands in their pockets, touching themselves. They can't stop doing it. And if you don't stop doing that filthy thing, you won't be able to control yourself. You'll become addicted to it."

For weeks I was obsessed by Mum's warning. I did not want to turn into one of those old men downtown who leans over the curb and presses a finger against one nostril and blows snot out of the other into a gutter. I challenged my willpower by setting goals of how many hours I could last without doing the thing. I challenged myself to go a whole day without. But less than an hour after the pledge, I went to the bathroom where a magazine was open to a page with an advertisement showing a naked woman lying front down on a black velvet cloth. I do not know what the advertisement was trying to sell, but it surely grabbed my attention. The picture rendered my challenge an agonizing tribulation. I rationalized that if I touched it only once or twice, I could still avoid technical consummation. So, I played coming-to-the-edge… But I eventually slipped over the edge. Mum was right, I was doomed. My filthy addiction affected other members of my family. My sisters were no longer permitted to walk from their bedroom to the bathroom with only a bra and girdle on. They had to close the bathroom door when processing their faces in the mirror.

❧❧❧

"I don't believe it," Joanie said to Angelin. "Each month it's a different story. So, the story is no longer that a man's pee makes a woman pregnant, but rather other stuff is squirted. And that's what makes a woman have a baby? And what did you call it?

"Sperm," Angelin said.

I wrote the word "spurm" in my tablet with the intention of looking it up in the encyclopedia later. "Who told you this stuff?" I asked.

"A ninth-grader in chorus showed me in her science book. This really is true."

I stood up and walked over to the window. I contemplated, {*I am not a freak of nature like the derelicts downtown. The things that happened to me this spring were maybe supposed to happen. Maybe other guys are experiencing the same … excitement, but have not said anything because it is just too weird. Or maybe they are ashamed because it involves a taboo area. Maybe, if I had some close friends who were boys, I could have traded stories and figured it out.*}

❧❧❧

I purposefully walked Angelin home because I wanted to talk to her. I said, "I need to ask you something."

"You mean you are not walking me home out of chivalry? I knew you wanted to talk, so shoot."

"Do you ever feel uncontrollably excited?"

"Uncontrollably?" a puzzled Angelin repeated.

"Take the ten best things you like—black raspberry ice cream, bubble baths, hearing that school is closed because of snow, whatever. Take all of those things combined, is there a feeling that you get for a few minutes that shocks your body, makes you shudder and feels better than everything else combined?"

"I've never felt anything that intense. What are you talking about?"

"Do you ever touch yourself, you know, like down there?"

"Every time I pee I wipe with TP afterwards. After a bath, I guess I wipe there some with a towel. Why?"

"Do you ever feel an uncontrollable urge to touch yourself?"

"No-o-o-o?"

"I think I have figured out some things, but not everything. For example, I understand why men are willing to have sex. They do it because it feels good—really, really good. Remember when I said that people must be willing to tolerate sex just once for each child? Well, now I think it probably happens a lot more often, maybe every day or every night."

"What? Now it's my turn to say that I don't believe it."

"Exactly, and that is the part I do not understand. I fully understand why guys want sex, but why do women do it? That is why I wanted to talk to you. I thought maybe you could shed some light on a woman's involvement."

Angelin shrugged and said, "I don't know, it all sounds pretty gross to me."

❧❧❧

On our first day in junior high school, Joanie and I had an hour session of study hall in the auditorium. Although we had nothing to study, we were entertained by gifted classmates who imitated sounds simulating barnyard animals. The participants were spread throughout the auditorium, giving the renditions the semblance of a conversation.

At the end of study hall, Joanie and I joined the line of students in the main aisle leading to the auditorium exit. We were going to our separate gym classes. Jerry Stopanyak was in front of us in the line. As we walked up the aisle, an obese girl walked towards us on the other side of the aisle. She waddled slightly. I anticipated a tight fit when she would get to us. When the girl got to Jerry Stopanyak, the girl's hip slightly bumped him. Jerry deliberately and dramatically threw himself across four seats along a row, as if he were hit by a meteor. As Jerry's head rose above the seats, he quickly looked around to make sure he had everyone's attention and to make sure he was collecting all of the recognition for which he hoped his adolescent funny yielded. At the moment, Jerry was concerned about what everyone in the auditorium thought about him and had no concern for the feelings of the obese girl. He did not know, and did not care, how deeply embarrassed and hurt she felt. She called him an ass. Jerry looked back at Joanie and asked, "Did you hear what Kong woman said? She called me an ass. I ask you, am I an ass?"

Joanie shrugged and said, "I don't know. According to an old Arab saying, if one person calls you an ass, ignore him. But if five persons call you an ass, then you'd better buy a saddle. Why don't you survey the people behind me."

A gifted member of the study hall barnyard chorus responded with a quality, "Hee-haww, hee-hah, hee-hah!"

Sixty guys were in my gym class. Like I, half were inexperienced seventh graders. Half were in eighth grade. For the first day, we sat on bleachers while the teacher gave an introduction to the course. He said, "For each class, you bring a towel, white tee-shirt, white sneakers, white socks, white gym trunks and a jock strap. Are there any questions?" I looked around the bleachers, hoping that someone else would ask the question because I did not want to take the lead. But no one raised a hand. I reluctantly raised mine and asked, "What is a jock strap?" The gallery burst out laughing, including the seventh graders sitting on both sides of me.

The teacher chuckled and said, "Well, you better not ask your sister." The strange thing was—the teacher never answered the question. When he dismissed the class, I still did not know what a jock strap was.

As we walked out of the gym, I asked one of the kids who sat beside me. He replied, "I dunno."

"But you were laughing with everyone else. Why would you laugh if you did not know what a jock strap was either? You were laughing when you did not even know the punch line."

"You gotta laugh when everyone else is laughing or you look like you don't know. I would've looked stupid… like you."

"For pity sake, you mean that I am responsible to wear something for class, and I do not even know what it is?" I did not want to ask anyone in my family. So, I asked the one person whom I knew would give me the straight poop. I asked Angelin. Thank you.

Chapter IX

The girls and I were at Joanie's house watching the movie, *Casablanca*, on the television. Just as the movie came to the final scene at the airport, Joanie's dad entered the parlor. He looked at the television and expressed, "Gee whiz, that picture sure is fuzzy." He went over to the set and, while partially blocking the screen, started fiddling with the tuning and contrast knobs. The picture and sound oscillated from slightly fuzzy to very fuzzy to unrecognizable and back again. He gave a full crank of the antenna rotary control that set atop the console. The rotary made an electric motor on the roof slowly rotate the antenna. The reception waned and improved and waned again.

I shook my head in dismay and muttered to Joanie through the corner of my mouth, "For crying out loud, can you not make him stop?"

"Daddy, we're watching the movie. Can't you do this later?"

"I'm just trying to make it better for you, Honey."

"But Daddy!" Joanie's dad finally quit *fixing* the television just when Bogey and Claude Raines were strolling down the foggy runway. The picture was about the same quality as before Joanie's dad had started adjusting the controls. He walked out of the room. After all the interference, he did not even stay to watch the television.

I picked up my Mason jar of cold tea and toasted Joanie, "Here's looking at you, kid." I took a swig of tea.

"Let's go to the junior high Christmas dance at the Ukrainian Club," Angelin blurted out of the blue. "It starts in about an hour."

"What brought that up?" Joanie whined. "Do you really want to go?"

"I've been thinking about it for a while. I've been in the junior high for a year and a half, and I've never been to a dance. I'd like to see what it's like. Who knows? Maybe a cute guy will ask me to dance." I was surprised because I had never heard her express a romantic interest. Angelin grinned, which made her under-bite all the more prominent. I cared a lot for Angelin, yet I still could not help but think, {*I do not know the standards at a junior high dance, yet I would not bet the farm on her chances of being asked to dance by anyone other than possibly by me.*}

Mary Jane asked, "May I go, too?" She was in the fifth grade but was small enough to look like she was in third.

"You have to be in junior high to get in," Joanie said.

"I do not think it is fair of you guys to abandon me tonight," Mary Jane protested.

"You can't expect us to pass up a dance just for you, do ya?" Angelin countered.

"Whoa," I said, "You and Joanie go. I will stay with Mary Jane."

"No, you have to go," Angelin insisted to me. "If no one else dances with us, you will have to."

"I do not know how to dance that rock and roll stuff," I cautioned.

"You just bounce to the beat," Joanie said.

I looked at Mary Jane who drooped with rejection. I asked, "Isn't there some way to get Mary Jane in?" Angelin and Joanie shrugged. I looked around the room. A pair of crutches standing in an umbrella rack in the corner of the room caught my attention. Joanie's brother, Ralphy, had used them when he had torn ligaments in his knee. "Mary Jane can come with us ... on crutches."

"I am not going to a junior high dance on crutches!" Mary Jane cried.

"How do crutches make her a junior high student?" Joanie queried.

"Because ... because ... Mary Jane has a childhood disease that has stunted her growth," I rationalized.

Joanie buried her face into her hands, rubbed her eyes and chided, "Daniel, you're crazy. That would never work."

"I am not going to the dance on crutches!"

"I think it would work," I said. "Imagine yourself as a teacher-chaperone at the door. The polio poster child comes hobbling to the door accompanied by three kids who definitely are in junior high. Do you make the poor little girl feel crummier than she already feels by asking her age, implying that you might not let her in? What would be the risk to letting her in?"

"Daniel's right," Angelin said. "The most important job of the chaperones is to prevent creepy older guys from getting in. The chaperones will even hold the doors open for her."

"I am not going to a junior high dance on crutches!"

"Take it or leave it, girl," I offered. "Look, you use the crutches only to get in. Once we are inside, we will stash them in the cloakroom… If you come, I will dance with you."

"How many dances?" Mary Jane asked.

I glanced at Joanie and Angelin. I shrugged and replied, "A third of them." I fetched the crutches and stood them beside Mary Jane to check the fit. I adjust the pins down four notches and tendered the crutches to Mary Jane to try on.

Angelin muffled her mouth with the palm of her hand and muttered, "My God, she does look like the polio poster child."

ॐॐॐ

There were no other seventh grade boys at the dance and only a few seventh grade girls, including Joanie. Only a few girls were dancing, and they were eighth and ninth graders. No guys were dancing. All of the guys were standing along walls, holding paper cups containing cherry pop. I felt too self-conscious to dance, especially since no other guys were dancing. While congregated in a foursome along a wall, one by one, the girls began moving to the music. Soon, I felt more self-conscious about standing perfectly still than I would have by shifting my weight to the beat in a sort-of semi-dance. We established a mini auxiliary dance floor along the wall. Since I was still standing against the wall, I felt comfortable that I had not committed to displaying myself as a dancer. The girls made goofy gestures to the beat and goaded me to mimic them. During one song, Joanie was positioned right in front of me. Although the music was rock and roll, she adapted a rock step that seemed to work. I mimicked her rock step. She waived her right hand for me to clasp, which I did. Only a few rock steps were required for me to reflexively raise my left hand that held Joanie's right hand. Joanie instinctively went into an underarm turn which drew us a few feet away from the wall. I led her through a repertoire of swing dance maneuvers. Near the end of the song, I returned to earth and noticed that Joanie and I were alone on the dance floor with the whole hall staring at us. One girl from the other end squealed, "Wooh!" and clapped.

Another song started. Mary Jane jumped out, saying "I am next. You promised." Mary Jane was fun to watch dancing the swing. She did an extra wiggle between beats that made her appear to be dancing twice as fast. She got lost in her dancing as if it temporarily obliterated from her consciousness the reality of her crummy life at home. While we laughed and tried catching our breath at the end of the song, a slow song immediately followed. Mary Jane looked at me and blushed. Two guys followed to the dance floor the two best looking girls in the hall, which made me feel more comfortable about staying on the floor. As we started to sway to the music, I glanced back at Angelin and Joanie. No one had asked them to dance. Early into the song, Mary Jane wiggled her right hand free of my clasp. She smiled subtly and held her hand up with her palm flat and facing me like an Indian chief would while saying "HOW". Guessing Mary Jane's intention, I listened to the rhythm of the music and decided that, with creative interpretation, it was possible. I placed the flat palm of my left hand against her right. With a slight push of the hand, I signaled that within a split second I would drive my left leg directly into her. She caught the cue and responded as we started the rhumba. All three girls were good dancers, but I enjoyed the rhumba with Mary Jane the best. She had flair. Whenever her left hand was free, she extended it to her side and behind her, making a sweeping, flowing movement like a wave. The movement gave Mary Jane grace and style. Again, all eyes were on us, and especially, Mary Jane.

As I should have expected, I spent the remainder of the evening on the floor doing a round-robin with Angelin, Joanie and Mary Jane. Near the end of the event, a gorgeous girl approached me and asked if I would teach her how to dance. By the maturity of her face and the size of her rack (a term I had just learned in the locker room), I judged her to have been a ninth grader. Mary Jane responded with lightening speed, saying "no way".

Angelin responded more forcefully by taking a step that planted her directly between the rack and me. Angelin declared, "I've been promised the dances for the rest of the evening." The statement was not true. Angelin glared back at Joanie who looked dumbfounded and remained to my left and a step behind me. Angelin tossed her head as a gesture for Joanie to do her duty and to anchor the left flank of the skirmish line. Joanie complied and took two steps forward.

"Well, maybe some other time," the ninth grader said as she retreated.

↭↭↭

Angelin was a smart girl who studied for her classes. But she was obstinate with her teachers. So, few, if any, teachers gave her the benefit of the doubt. When another student got an "A" or a "B" for a given achievement, Angelin received a "C" for a similar performance. Joanie tried to explain to her that swimming upstream was inefficient, unproductive and exhausting. Angelin already understood the problems she caused for herself, but her nature refused to yield to authority.

Earlier in the week, Angelin's English teacher caught her gazing out of a classroom window at a boy's gym class running around the parking lot in the rain. The teacher sternly repeated for Angelin the vocabulary question, "What is the definition of the word *scud*?"

Having had studied her vocabulary assignment, Angelin knew that the verb form of scud meant to run or skim along swiftly and easily—as clouds would. Angelin sniffed as she wiped her nose with the back of her hand and said, "Scud? It's a mixture of scum and mud." Angelin's response royally honked off the teacher.

⤳⤳⤳

One spring day when I was in eighth grade, Mum told me she wanted to discuss an important matter with me. I was immediately apprehensive because Mum rarely discussed anything with me, let alone an important matter. The last time we had had a serious conversation, Mum was touching my crotch feeling for masturbation wetness. I could only assume that either a family member was seriously ill or I had perpetrated an egregious offense of which I was clueless.

"Daniel, I think you should consider going to school next year at Salzburg Prep." Wow, she sure surprised me. I had no idea she was thinking about a prep school for me. She probably had been thinking about it for a long time. I had to give her credit. Mum never shot from the hip when a major decision had to be made. She also must have discussed this with Dad many times.

"Why?" I asked.

"Salzburg Prep is a good school."

"I am learning stuff in junior high. There are six sections in eighth grade, and I am in eight-one. Next year I will take French and algebra. Carolyn scored in the fifteen hundreds on the college boards having gone through this system. How much higher of a score do you want?"

"Rich people send their sons to Salzburg Prep. It's important to make connections with people who are rich and powerful."

"That school has to be thirty minutes away. Who would drive me there every day?" I did not tell Mum, but I had stumbled across the school on one of my mammoth bicycle excursions. Salzburg Prep sets on a bluff above the Kiskiminetas River, surrounded by pine trees. It was about twenty-five miles away.

You would live there … in a dormitory."

"What! But I do not know anyone there." I stared out the window, my eyes widening as I contemplated the implications. "What about my customers? What about my friends?" I meant—what about the girls?

"You would benefit by having some male friends. Maybe you would be less … active."

"Hearing the guys' banter in the locker room at the gym just a few minutes each week leads me to believe that the girls are a moderating influence on me."

"Maybe you'll meet a nice sister or cousin of one of the boys at the prep school."

"Why a sister or cousin? Why would I not meet a girl in my classes?"

"Ah, there aren't any girls at Salzburg Prep. It's a prep school for boys."

"What!?" I thought, {No looking down Kimberly's blouse when she leans over to erase a mark on her paper, no watching while Donna's jumper shimmies up her thighs each time she fidgets in her seat, no opportunity for the inevitable full beaver shot.} "How much will they pay to compensate me for such deprivation?"

"Pay you? Don't be ridiculous, Daniel. We pay the school. Private schools cost a lot of money."

"This does not make any sense. Here, I dwell in the land of milk and honey. Yet, I would have to pay them to have me banished to the barren wasteland? I presume that the guy who developed this idea has been duly committed to an insane asylum."

I did not completely reject the idea of prep school until that night after fully considering the ramifications. First, I hated those preppy guys. And at Salzburg, there was no Pooza to gas them to their senses. But the deal breaker was the money. It would have been different if my folks were independently wealthy. But my mum was a housewife, and my dad was a lathe roll turner in a heavy foundry. He was an expert in shaping monster rolls used as machinery in steel and aluminum rolling mills. He was the highest paid union worker in the foundry. But he was still a laborer. My folks had five kids. I could have taken the total cost of that snooty school and divided it by my dad's hourly wage rate to estimate the number of hours my dad would have had to sweat at the foundry to send me there. My parents could have made the payments simply because they were prepared to tighten the belt to any extent necessary to achieve the goal. And that is why I did not enroll at Salzburg Prep. I had no problem with making a commitment and assuming a challenge. But it had to be my sacrifice, not someone else's. If I were paying the price, then if I chose to bust my ass one day and goof-off the next, then I would have been satisfied with my choices. As a typical teenager, sometimes I would have wanted to goof-off. But if I chose to blow-off one day while I knew that my parents were sacrificing to send me to that God-forsaken place, the guilt would have been unbearable.

Chapter X

On the second Sunday of May when I was in ninth grade (the last month of junior high school), I was at Angelin's house replacing the ribbon on her Smith-Corona typewriter.

"Daniel, could you do me a big favor?"

"I am already doing you a big favor."

"I have a birthday at the end of the month. My extended family has a huge reunion on Memorial Day. Thousands of people come… Well, OK, would you believe fifty?"

"Yea, I remember last year," I said. "I was there."

"Then you should remember how my folks use part of the festivities to celebrate my birthday. One of the extended attendees will be my cousin, Carmen."

"I cannot stand that girl," I said with a grimace.

"Tell me about it. I hate that loud-mouthed snot rag. We're both sophomores at Kiski Area High. So, I have to look at her ugly face every day. Because we're the same age, our families have always tried to match us up as bosom buddies. So, what we really have fostered has been a competition to the death."

"What does all of this have to do with me?"

"Carmen's got a boyfriend. He's a junior named Terry. Everywhere she goes, every time I see her, it's 'oh Terry this and oh Terry that'. She makes me want to gag canned spam. She is so into having a boyfriend … and the fact that I don't. She flaunts him in front of me, that zit-faced, grease head at every opportunity.

"And you want me to do what?"

"I want you to come to my birthday party on Memorial Day."

"Sure, OK. I went last year. So did Mary Jane and Joanie."

"I want you to come to it alone." Angelin pivoted in her chair so as to stare directly at me. "I want you to pretend to be my boyfriend." We sat in silence while Angelin gave me time to contemplate her proposal. She understood the issues with which I would be grappling. I had no problem with the idea of posing as Angelin's beau. I would gladly have her benefit from my playing the role. Also, the intrigue of the deception whetted my devilish appetite. But the real issue, as Angelin well knew, was Joanie and Mary Jane. Joanie would be honked off, but Mary Jane would go absolutely ballistic. I had never dated just one girl. It had always been Daniel for all, and all three for Daniel. While I had felt an attraction for each, especially cute little Mary Jane, I had never manifested favoritism for one over the others. I had always treated them with equality. Memorial Day would have been a typical group holiday when the triplets and I would hang out and do something together. To Mary Jane and Joanie, the idea of presenting myself as Angelin's boyfriend to a group of people, even in jest, and excluding Mary Jane and Joanie from the party, would fly as successfully as a lead zeppelin.

To Angelin's surprise, I did not confront the main issue. I attempted an end run, instead. "I am a freshman in junior high. If you want to upstage Carmen, would not a boyfriend from Kiski High be more prestigious?"

"You only have a month left in junior high. Besides, I need to be brutally frank with myself. The guys at the Big K are not exactly tripping over each other to get in line to ask me out."

Angelin's revelation was funny, honest, profound, self-deprecating and sad. "I cannot believe there is no one whom you could recruit at the high school."

"Well, yea, there's this one guy. But look, Daniel, Carmen's Terry is a gangly, ugly nerd. I don't want to just match her with my version of a gangly, ugly nerd. I want to trump her. I want to show up with … a really good-looking guy."

I was astounded by Angelin's assessment of me. Mum had called me handsome. But I thought that she was dutifully, maternally lying, or perhaps her judgment was impaired, just like Mrs. Marzetti next door. My neighbor honestly believed she had the cutest baby on earth. But I swear on my honour that that was the ugliest baby I had ever seen. "OK, I will play the part, but why must you not invite Joanie and Mary Jane to the party and let them know about the prank?"

"Come on, be realistic with both of us. I place my hand through your arm and introduce you as my BOYFRIEND to an assembly of fifty people. What would Mary Jane do?"

"She would go frick'n berserk," I said resignedly.

"Exactly."

࿓࿓࿓

Shortly after Angelin and I arrived at Joanie's house, Angelin alleviated the tension she felt by making a phone call to the corner grocery. Using a housewife's voice, Angelin asked the grocer, "Do you have Prince Albert in a can?" She was referring to a brand of chewing tobacco sold in a tin can.

"I don't think I've run out," the shopkeeper said. "Let me check the shelf." Angelin could hear him walk to the far end of the counter where he must have scanned the shelf opposite of the counter. Angelin heard the shopkeeper walk back to the phone and pick up the receiver. "Yuppers, I have Prince Albert in a can."

"Then you better let him out."

"Damn it, lady. I'm a busy man trying to make a living …" Click—Angelin hung up.

"OK," Angelin said to me. "Now I'm loose enough to talk about my birthday party. So, Daniel, tell them about the plan."

"Moi?" I was unprepared to initiate the certain conflict. I almost volleyed back to Angelin when I considered that I may be able to put a more unobjectionable spin on her proposal. "Angelin has an idea for playing the best prank on her cousin, Carmen."

"Yuck," Joanie said. "She's the most self-centered, selfish brat I've ever met."

I made a good start describing the plan. Joanie and Mary Jane were enthusiastic. Within a few minutes, however, their attitudes changed completely. Mary Jane's face flushed, and a vein in her neck protruded. I came to realize that any attempt to give the plan a positive spin was futile. Joanie said with punctuated speech, "I knew she would eventually try to claim you. Bottom line, you are telling me that she's your girlfriend and I'm just a friend."

"You are much more than just a friend," I pleaded. "I care for all of you, equally."

"Bullshit!" Mary Jane yelled as she dropkicked a gigantic brown can of potato chips that had just been home-delivered. Potato chips spewed everywhere. "You are declaring in front of God and everyone that Angelin is your girlfriend."

"Well," I blurted to Mary Jane in angst. "I will just have to declare in front of everyone that you are my girlfriend." The room went silent. I had no idea where I was going to go with the promise I had just made. I had said it in panic.

Angelin whispered forcefully, "You are declaring what?"

"Shooosh," I snapped back. "You started this mess. Now, I am going to put out this firestorm."

"Where will you declare me your girlfriend?" Mary Jane asked with eyes ablazed in anger.

"In front of all the seventh graders. You know that puffy V—letter that I got for placing second in the broad jump at the regional track meet? It has a fake gold pin on it in the form of track shoes with wings on them? I will give you the letter and let you sew it onto one of your sweaters."

"That is it?" Mary Jane was not impressed.

"I will buy you a matching beret… Your locker is at the alley end of the seventh grade corridor. Five minutes early each day, I will walk you around the block to the front entrance of the junior high. Wearing the track letter on your sweater and the beret, you may hold my arm as I, a ninth grader, escort you down the entire seventh grade hallway, past everyone's locker. I will do that everyday until the end of the school year." Mary Jane went catatonic. "Mary Jane … Mary Jane? Breath, Mary Jane. Is it a deal?"

"Deal!" gasped Mary Jane.

"Whatever you give me, it better be good," Joanie said with an impish grin.

"OK, I will exclusively take you to see *The Music Man* performance at Kiski."

"Oooh, I like," Joanie cooed.

"Oh no, I wanted to see *The Music Man*," Angelin cried.

"Me too," Mary Jane moaned.

"Do you want me to take back my promises?" I admonished them. Angelin and Mary Jane sheepishly shook their heads.

Joanie said, "I don't think this is fair. Mary Jane gets the grand entrance every school day this month. You are promising to take me out only one crummy night."

"OK, I will take you to eat at DJ's diner before."

"Add taking me to mass this Sunday, and it's a deal."

I laughed as I thought, {*Mum will get a charge out of this. She is honked off because I refuse to go to church with the family. Now, I will be going with Joanie to the Slovak church.*}

"Wait a minute," Angelin said, "You can't take Joanie to the Kiski musical. What if Carmen is there and sees you?"

"You will have to find out if she is going, and if so, then to which performance."

"How do I find that out?" Angelin asked.

"Ask Carmen. Be subtle. Tell her you were thinking of going to the musical. Better yet, have your mother talk to Carmen's mother." I tilted back in my chair almost to the point of losing balance as I contemplated all the promises I had made. My life was about to become more complicated and exhausted.

ఎఎఎ

The royal promenade every morning took forever. Mary Jane acted like an outgoing bride as she stopped every couple of feet to wave, greet and talk to friends. I did not mind, however, pretending to be Mary Jane's boyfriend. She was blond and cute as a button. Not only did all of the girls check us out, so did the boys. The eyes of the boys were fixed on Mary Jane. A few coveted the letter sported on her sweater. But most were coveting pretty Mary Jane.

I also enjoyed playing the role of boyfriend at Angelin's birthday party / family reunion. I thought perhaps I should audition for high school plays because I enjoyed acting so much. Angelin wore a new outfit. Her top was white and made of rows of bulging elastic cords that expanded and contracted to the body's contour. The top made her boobs appear enormous. Everyone treated me well, especially Angelin's parents. "Level-headed boy" was the way her father described me. I was not Italian, but I was Catholic, or so they presumed. Mostly, I believed that Angelin's folks were relieved that I was not as dorky as their niece's boyfriend. When Angelin's oldest uncle bemoaned that I was not Italian, I goodheartedly responded, "No, but I have been talking to a priest about converting to Italian." A record player provided music during most of the reunion. Some of the records were in Italian, which I did not mind. At least you can dance to the Italian music. Angelin's youngest sister followed me around all afternoon. The six-year-old stood on my feet while I danced with her. Carmen asked me to dance. Angelin hated the idea but acted graciously in front of her extended family. While my left palm and Carmen's right palm were adjoined, she covertly slid her middle finger repeatedly up and down the middle of my palm. I did not know why she wished to tickle my palm. It was not until ten years later, while reminiscing with a mug of stout in hand, that I realized that Carmen had been conveying a message. Thank goodness, I was too naïve at the time to have understood the proposition. My life was too complicated already to have endured the additional damage potentially resulting from consorting with Carmen. As disgusting as Carmen was, a proposition to a virginal boy would have been deemed too providential to have refused.

When I escorted Joanie on Sunday, it was the first time I had been in church since I had lost my faith years earlier. I had been in church hundreds of times, yet it seemed that morning with Joanie like I was entering a church for the first time. As in my Polish church, the babushkas with prune-like faces, clothed in black from head to foot, lined the back of the church. Each babushka was in her own world, saying the rosary over and over again. They were oblivious to the mass being celebrated. While the babushkas were technically not saying the rosary out loud, they unconsciously audibilized a plethora of "sh" and "ch" sounds so prevalent in the Slavic languages. Collectively, they produced a cacophony. It occurred to me that many of the girls for whom I lusted in class were genetically descended from those grotesque creatures.

The statues of the Blessed Virgin and Saint Joseph did not look Jewish. They had reddish tint in the hair and hazel eyes that made them look Irish. I looked at the stained glass windows, the candles, the heavy ornate lanterns, the chalice, the geometric patterns of the arched supports in the ceiling, the protruding ribs of the nearly naked Jesus, the powdery smoke of incense arising. During the hundreds of times I had seen them before, they had exuded a reality beyond my world. At that moment, however, they were mere … things. Some were artistic, some were gaudy, and some were ridiculous. The priest was a man just like all men with a receding hairline. He was an émigré from the old country whose accent made him sound like Count Dracula, especially when he said, "Da blood… da blood of the everlasting covenant that was shed for you and all mankind…" I felt eerie being in the church. I was a stranger in a strange place, like a detached anthropologist observing a tribal ritual.

Chapter XI

The high school sophomore dance was on the Saturday night after Angelin's birthday. The gym was still decorated from the prom a week earlier. To the consternation of Mary Jane and Joanie, Angelin asked me to the sophomore dance and I accepted. Joanie and Mary Jane's protestations muted, though, as they realized the claims each had acquired when she would become a sophomore in her turn.

The Tuesday after the sophomore dance was the last day of school and also the Kiski Area school picnic. At the defunct Vandergrift train station, the girls and I boarded the special train bound for the amusement park an hour away, near Pittsburgh. The train ride was as much fun as any of the amusement park rides. None of us had ever before been on a train. As we climbed down from the train, a school chaperone shouted repeatedly, "Always remember to mind your P's and Q's."

"What does she mean when she says 'mind your P's and Q's'?" Joanie asked.

"That was a term used in feudal days when noblemen went hunting," Angelin replied. "The king's chancellor gave a prize to the nobleman who bagged the greatest number of pheasants and quail during a hunting outing. But to win, you had to mind your P's and Q's."

"Oh," Joanie muttered. Angelin rolled her eyes in tribute to Joanie's gullibility.

At the park, we quickly exhausted our supply of discount tickets for the rides we had purchased two weeks earlier. Angelin berated me for being so cheap as to have not purchased enough tickets back at school. I had made a conservative estimate because I could not stand the thought of the day ending and my still having unused tickets. I was not about to purchase the exorbitantly priced tickets sold at the park.

So, to stop the girl's bellyaching, I suggested taking a ride in a rowboat in the pond surrounded by the amusement park. The rowboats did not take ride tickets, but cost forty cents for a half-hour. Split among four, the price was reasonable. When we got into the boat, we opened the package of red wax lips we had purchased at a novelty booth. We each wore a pair of lips using clenched teeth to hold them in place. As a complement to her lips, Joanie put on a pair of sunglasses. I was a cheapskate, but I would have paid any price to have had a picture of us four in that rowboat wearing our lips. Joanie and Angelin sat on the middle seat, each working an opposing oar. They could not, however, coordinate their strokes. So, we weaved left and right uncontrollably. Mary Jane, who sat in the front, yelled, "Watch out, we are going to hit those guys in front of us."

Sitting in the back, I stomped the bottom of the wooden boat with the rhythm of a pace-keeper on a Roman warship powered by galley slaves at the oars. "Ramming speed," I barked in a low-pitched, authoritative voice.

"We are going to h…!" The impact threw the girls onto the bottom. I was nearly catapulted into the drink and would have been, if I had not braced for the impact. While Joanie slid off the seat, a wood splinter imbedded into the back of her thigh, pretty high up. Poor Joanie, her thighs were injury prone. She should have worn long pants. I took charge of both oars and rowed back to the dock. Standing by a bench, Joanie pulled up the back cuff of her shorts and tilted forward slightly. Angelin, Mary Jane and I crouched to evaluate the splinter. Luckily, a little bit of the splinter appeared close to the entry point. One of us could remove it.

"Do you want me to try to take it out?" I asked. Joanie appeared reluctant as she looked back at me. After all, I was a guy. She glanced at Mary Jane, then Angelin, and then back at me. After all of our years together, on the continuum between Florence Nightingale and sex fiend, Joanie did not know quite where to place me.

"OK, Daniel. Get it out."

I pinched the root with the fingernails of one hand to prevent the splinter from digging any deeper. Using the thumbnail of the other hand, I pressed her skin about two inches from the splinter and slid the thumbnail towards the splinter in an attempt to get the nail deeply under the head of the splinter. With my index fingernail, I vice-clenched the splinter and pulled it out, cleanly—to the extent I was able to see.

A loudspeaker announced the commencement in five minutes of a high-wire and swinging acrobats show. We walked a short distance to the bridge that spanned a narrow water passage connecting the two main bodies of the rowboat pond. The arching bridge was the best location from which to watch the show. A high wire and swings were stretched across the pond. A banner hanging from the main performer platform announced, "Les Triplés" (Lay-twree-play). Les Triplés were two men and a woman wearing a very revealing outfit. They were very athletic. The woman spun on a wire for half a minute, supported by only a mouthpiece clasped in her teeth. During the remainder of the day, I collectively called Mary Jane, Joanie and Angelin—Les Triplés.

During the performance, Stefan Strelzyck, a classmate, approached me offering to sell two books of ride tickets at the face value of two dollars per book. "Wow!" I exclaimed. "How many tickets did you bring with you?"

"Two books, that's all. I've spent all day at the ski-ball trying to win a stuffed gorilla." Every year, Strelzyck bought books of ride tickets, but never used them. The kid was hooked on ski-ball and the novelty gifts he could purchase through redemption of ski-ball tickets, won by achieving distinct score levels. All day long he had been pumping nickels into the ski-ball. A nickel inserted into the machine released eight duckpin-sized balls that Strelzyck rolled up an inclined alley. A steeply raised lip at the end of the runway caused the ball to go airborne. Depending upon the ball speed and the stroke of the player, the ball would fall into one of the holes of differing difficulty. The machine kept tally of the score and, at the end of the game, dispensed prize-redeemable ticket awards. Strelzyck did not detach from the machine the tickets won from only one game, but rather let the tickets, each of which was attached to the next ticket, accumulate into ribbons of tickets measuring yards in length. As he spoke to me, his left hand clutched coiled ribbons of tickets won earlier. In a store outside of the park, the prize Strelzyck sought could not cost more than ten percent of the nickels he fed into the machine. I could not fathom why Strelzyck disgorged a fortune on a nearly worthless novelty. Perhaps the novelty was a perverse symbol of personal achievement, visible for everyone to see, especially his parents. Unquestionably, though, Strelzyck's folks must have had more money than brains to have provided the support that enabled the obsession. "Do ya wanna buy the ride books or not?" Strelzyck blurted with a sense of urgency.

"I do not know," I said. I casually waived my hand in the direction of the sun. "It is getting pretty late. We might not have enough time to use all of the tickets before we have to board the train." Angelin glared at me. "Tell you what," I said. "I will give you two dollars for both books." Angelin rolled her eyes and turned her head away from me.

"But I paid four bucks for the ride tickets."

"I know," I said as I again waived towards the sun. "But I would be assuming the risk of running out of time while still holding unused tickets."

"The four of you could use up the tickets quick."

"I am not so sure. Joanie just got a splinter up her butt. Who knows how many more rides she can last. By the way, how many more ski-ball tickets do you need?"

"Seventy-four," Strelzyck said with precision.

"Well, two bucks is a whole roll of nickels, forty nickels. Can you average winning two ski-ball tickets per game?"

"Ah, it's a piece of cake," Stefan Strelzyck replied with the arrogance of an insulted, professional ski-ball roller.

"Well, there it is," I said as I pulled from my pocket a fistful of crumpled dollar bills. I could have easily selected two of the many one-dollar bills, but I fished out the sole two-dollar bill just for its visual impact. I held up the two-dollar bill and said, "The gorilla is within your grasp. You just have to seize it." Strelzyck slapped the ticket books into my other hand and snatched the two-dollar bill. Without saying "good bye", he bolted in the direction of the ski-ball.

The park was built on an escarpment about eight hundred feet of vertical drop above the Monongahela River. The train was in the valley at river level. I muttered to myself, "Thank goodness we climbed the cindered trail up to the park when we arrived in the morning, and now we can leisurely coast back down to leave." As les triplés and I selected a pair of mutually facing seats on the train, I saw Strelzyck at the end of our car with the gorilla sitting beside him. Five minutes into the ride, Joanie started to unravel layers of the cotton candy she held on a rolled paper stick. After ten minutes of the train swaying, she sprang towards the window and frantically worked the latches and opened it. Joanie stuck her face out the window as far as she could while up-chucking the reconstituted pink syrup. Unfortunately, the train was moving fifty miles per hour and all of the kids downwind of us had their windows open.

↭↭↭

As sophomores entering high school, Joanie and I were again able to have lunches with Angelin who was a junior. But it would be two years until Mary Jane would be able to join us. Joanie and I were in the same academic program for the college-bound, so we had the same schedule of classes. The only time I did not see Joanie was when she and Angelin had chorus together. I would have loved to have been in the chorus, but I was tone deaf. An attempt by me to sing was comical. I was so bad that my best effort sounded like a movie parody of a person purposefully attempting to sound bad.

On Friday of the first week of school, I waited to rendezvous with Joanie at the stairway to the cafeteria. I soon discovered that the bottom of the stairway was a strategically ideal spot from which to watch girls as they ascended the steps.

"Hey!" Joanie barked while poking me in the ribs from behind, startling me. "I've been watching you looking up girls' skirts as they walk up the steps. You should be ashamed of yourself."

"I...I...I..." Embarrassed because the indictment was true, my first reaction was to deny the charge. However, it was also my nature to immediately ask myself why I committed the transgression. Just then Kimberly walked by and gave me a smile. I watched as she climbed the stairs. I murmured, "Sweet mother of pearl." I also realized that Joanie's accusation was unjustified. I looked at Joanie. I took a step back from her so that I could survey, by moving my eyes, the whole outfit she was wearing. "Nice shoes you have," I said while nodding my head. Joanie's shoes had two-inch heels, not narrow, but they did stretch her legs two more inches. "Are your shoes good for hiking?"

"Are you kidding? I can't wait to get home to change out of them. I have blisters at two different places from them."

"Did you buy those shoes because they were inexpensive?"

"I don't wear cheap shoes." Joanie huffed.

Joanie wore a skirt typical for a high school girl. It came to mid-thigh on her. "Did a male choose the clothes you wear?"

"No?"

"Did a helicopter from a relief agency drop a crate of skirts into your back yard?"

"No, my folks pay for my clothes, but I pick the outfits, within the limits of their price range, of course."

"Is your skirt good for raspberry picking or for digging coal?"

"No?"

"Does your skirt improve your ability to study? I sure as hell know that it impairs mine."

"Why are you asking such weird things?"

"I am just trying to determine the function of the clothes you wear. I know that your skirt is inconvenient to you. You cannot bend over normally in it. You constantly have to keep your legs together while you are sitting. That has to be uncomfortable because when I sit, my legs split apart naturally. You cannot even get in or out of a car normally. Honestly, I think it would be more useful for guys to wear skirts than it is for girls… You know, if you were one of those Muslim girls who wear tents over their bodies, then you might have a legitimate beef if a guy commits an indiscretion. If you were one of those Amish babes who wear high-top tennis shoes and loose fitting, ankle length dresses, then you would be justified in admonishing a guy for looking at you with prurient thoughts."

"But it's all about fashion," Joanie protested.

"Bullshit."

Chapter XII

At the crack of dawn on the first day of summer vacation, I headed on my bicycle for Ford City, a twenty-mile trek over many steep western Pennsylvania ridges. Ford City was a small town, yet two residents could not give me directions to the driver's license testing center of the Pennsylvania Department of Transportation. A gas station mechanic pointed down the street. I was but four blocks away from the center. Of the three desks in the center, only one was occupied. The name-plate in front of the uniformed trooper read, "Zigmund L. Mrasz." What luck, I thought.

"Dzien dobry, Officer Mrasz."

"Dzien dobry. Jak sie masz? Jak moge Ci pomagac?"

"I would like an application for a learner's permit, Officer."

"Where are your parents?"

"They are not with me. I have my birth certificate showing that I am sixteen." I unfolded the document that I had been holding and presented it to the trooper.

"I'm sorry, Daniel. But I can't issue a permit without a parent's signature giving permission on the application."

"I know. I just want an application form. If I have an application filled out and ready to go, I think I might have an easier time getting my dad to sign."

"Where do you live?"

"Vandergrift."

"Well, how did you…?"

"I rode my bike."

The trooper chuckled and said, "You're one crazy kid, Daniel." He opened a side drawer and drew a learner's permit application form.

Laying the form atop my birth certificate, the trooper handed both to me. "Be very careful on your ride home."

"Dziekuje, do widzenia, Officer Mrasz."

When I arrived home, I parked the bike in the garage and walked to Angelin's house. It felt good to simply walk after a full day in the saddle. I tossed the learner's permit application on the kitchen table near Angelin. "Wow-ee-wow, you're gonna get a driver's license?" Angelin cried.

"No," I relied. "I am not applying for a permit. *You* are."

Angelin flinched and said, "Me, why me?"

"Even when someone sixteen gets a license, he still may not drive unless an adult is in the car. And what good would that do for all of us?" Pointing to Angelin, I continued, "But a seventeen-year-old is allowed to drive until eleven at night without an adult. So, you get a license now, and I will get one next year."

"I don't know if my dad will sign this."

"You are not even going to ask him," I said. "I will sign his name."

"You could never duplicate his handwriting."

"I do not have to. The troopers at the license place do not know what your father's signature looks like. And they do not care. You are seventeen, and you look twenty. The troopers are not going to give you a hard time. Do you know where your birth certificate is?"

"Yeah. It's in a shoebox in the bottom of my folks' bedroom closet, along with the deed to the house and a bunch of other papers that I don't know what they are."

"When can you get it?"

"What if my folks see that it's missing?"

"For crying out loud, when was the last time your folks looked at your birth certificate? I bet it is on the bottom of the shoebox and your folks have not touched it since you were born. So, when do you think that you can get it?"

"Everyone is going to grandma's on Sunday. I'm supposed to go, but I probably can get out of it. The house will be empty."

"Good. We will go to the license place on Monday."

"Where is it?"

"Ford City."

"Who's taking us?"

"No one. We will ride there on bikes."

"Whoa, isn't Ford City a long ways?"

"Not too far. The ride is a piece of cake."

"Oh—OK, but I don't have a bike. Do you have a bike for me?"

"We will get Joanie's bike. I will oil the chain and pump the tires to slightly over the pressure capacity to get the max efficiency."

Angelin leaned on her elbows as she perused the form. "The permit costs five smackers. I don't have that." Instantaneously, I slapped a five spot onto the table. "You're going to pay for *my* learner's permit?"

"This is a group project," I answered.

જીજીજી

Halfway up the first ridge, Angelin huffed with exhaustion. "I don't think being able to drive myself to a summer stock theatre at a barn somewhere is worth all of this."

Worried that she would quit the endeavor, I grasped Angelin's bike and walked while pushing both bikes, each flanking me on opposite sides. I knew I had enough wind in me to reach the top, but I was concerned about my hands. To use but one hand to keep each bike aligned for moving forward and upward, each hand needed to exert a lot of pressure at the fulcrum of the handlebars to keep them from swerving. I did not know how long I could continue before my hands would start aching nor when the aching would become unbearable. "Your being able to drive provides us with more opportunities than just going to plays, swimming holes and dance lessons," I said. "You can drive us to take college courses next summer at IUP."

Angelin, who had been walking behind me, stopped and stared at me as I unknowingly got farther and farther ahead. "Hey. Hey! I'm taking a break." Angelin sat atop a truncated telephone pole used as an anchor to support the guardrail cable stretching to the next post. I stacked the bikes against the post two up from Angelin. I sat on the post next to her, about ten feet away. "You little worm," Angelin started. "I knew it. I could tell by how quick you were with the answers that you've been thinking too much. Group project—my eye." Angelin burst into laughter.

"I just think that we should be thinking about the end game, especially you. You are going to be a senior. Have you not thought about the future?"

"I thought if I ignored the future, it would go away. I just wanted to enjoy the summer. But why do you have a burr up your ass? You won't be graduating next summer."

"I do not want to waste next summer."

"Daniel, I have never seen you waste a minute, especially during summers. You are either working hard, or playing hard or sleeping."

"Yea, I work hard, and I make a lot of dough. But I am not progressing. I am mowing lawns, but I was mowing lawns and shoveling snow six years ago. It is time for a promotion. You are right, Angelin. I do have a burr up my ass."

"Don't you need a diploma from high school before going to college?"

"You do not have to meet any requirements if you enroll for some courses without being in a degree program. When I looked at the catalogs in the guidance counselor's office, all of the colleges require a core of a bunch of liberal arts courses. If we take the courses in that liberal arts core, we can apply them to any bachelor degree we choose at IUP, or we can transfer them to another college."

"Yea, but are we prepared enough, you know, intellectually to do college work?"

"Are you kidding?" I said. "Bucky Biola, the football player, scored seven hundred on the college boards. That is seven hundred total, not just on one part. He is going to a teachers' college, and he is an imbecile. He is not smart, like you."

My compliment made Angelin grin. "What are you gonna major in?"

"I do not know."

"You went through these elaborate plans, and you don't even know what you will major in? You talked about accounting."

"I really do not know," I said. "Accounting sounds really boring. How about you?"

"The only career I rule out is being a teacher. We might relish the pranks we pull on our teachers. But to the teachers it has got to be the most frustrating and demeaning job in the world."

"Teaching is the second most demeaning job. The worst job is school bus driver. How he puts up with the daily barrage of fruit, paper balls and insults hurled at him from that pack of animals, I will never understand. I would rather starve than drive a school bus."

"I was thinking of being a pharmacist," Angelin said. "I would not have to cut someone open or clean bedpans. Emergency calls in the middle of the night are rare. Pharmacists seem to make pretty good money just for counting pills."

"That sounds like a good career. I will be a pharmacist, too," I declared.

"No way!" Angelin chided. "That's my career. You find your own. Besides, there isn't enough room for two pharmacists in Vandergrift."

"What? You are planning on staying in Vandergrift?"

"Yea. Why do you ask?"

"Oh, no reason."

When we reached the summit, I suggested we take another break. A biker does not want to take a break when it would hinder momentum while racing downhill, momentum that could help in the ascent of the next hill. I pulled from my kitbag one of two insulated vacuum bottles of iced and sweetened tea. The kitbag had been my dad's during the war. I adjusted the straps so I could carry the bag as a small backpack. I offered Angelin a modest half of a cup-sized capful. I did not take a drink because we needed to conserve for the trip. Besides, I was not thirsty because I had purposefully drunk like a camel right before leaving home. If anything, I would soon need to drain the vein. I advised Angelin against breaking while going downhill. I explained, "On a long trip, you need to ride like a truck driver. You need to go like a bat out of hell downhill to build momentum for the next hill." After we again started to ride, midway on the downhill with no braking, I had to have exceeded fifty miles an hour. I thought, *{Maybe I* *should have brought a spare inner tube.}* Then I thought, {*If I have a blowout right now, I won't need a spare inner tube. The ambulance workers would need to use a spoon to collect my remains from this road.*}

"This is the craziest thing I've ever done," Angelin whined as we slogged up the next hill. I interpreted her words as a rebuke of my idea, which made me feel dejected. I hated criticism when I worked so hard to do the right thing.

As we entered Ford City, I asked Angelin how she was doing. She replied that she was going to write a book, titled <u>Twenty Years in the Saddle</u> by Major Assburn. When we got near the driver's license center, I told Angelin to stop a moment as I peeked around the edge of the front window. "There are two troopers in there," I reported. "One is Officer Mrasz. He seemed to be a fair guy. But even better, the other guy looks Italian. The Italian is occupied with someone. If you go in now, you will get Mrasz. Wait until Mrasz is busy so you get the paisano. By the way, I need to give you something." I pulled a Kiski High yearbook from my bag.

"For Pete's sake, if you had granted me a million attempts to guess what you had in your bag, I never would have gotten it."

"Most teenagers who walk into there have their parents with them. When you walk in there alone …"

"You're not going in with me?" Angelin asked.

"Officer Mrasz would recognize me and wonder what was going on. Anyway, going in there without a parent causes two problems. The trooper may question the authenticity of your dad's signature. Being alone looks suspicious. The second problem is the question of your identity and age. If an adult, who looks like he is related, accompanies the teenager, then a mere birth certificate seems like enough ID. We cannot do anything to improve the legitimacy of your dad's faked signature, but the yearbook can prove that you are you. The popsicle stick marks the page with your picture. So, here is the birth certificate that says "Angelin Bugliese" (Bull-yay-see), and there is the yearbook with your mug saying "Angelin Francesca Bugliese". Just how many Angelin Bugliese's can there be in Vandergrift?"

"Where are your parents, Miss?" the trooper asked.

"Neither could bring me, so my boyfriend … brought me." Angelin looked down and saw a large grease stain, from the bike chain, streaking across the inner cuff of the right leg of her beige pants. {*Sweet Jesus in heaven,*} she thought. "Look, my mama doesn't drive, and papa has a bad back from the steel mill. The drive to here would have killed his back. That's why I want to get a license—so that I can drive mama and grandma to the market and my little sister to piano lessons. It's important for me to relieve my papa as much as possible from the burden of driving."

Chapter XIII

Before leaving Ford City, we stopped at a corner grocery store. I bought Angelin a marshmallow snowball as a celebratory gift. She was giddy over her success in acquiring a learner's permit. I hoped the adrenaline would carry her through the exhausting trip home.

"How am I going to explain this permit to my folks?" Angelin asked.

"Again, that is simple," I answered. "You will not tell them. We will get my dad to teach you how to drive. You have to wait three months to take the test. That is September. We do not want to waste my dad's time, so you will take only a few lessons, and they will be in late August to maximize the experience right before the exam. And August is when we will ask Dad to give you the lessons."

"Why would *your* dad be willing to give *me* lessons?"

"I will just plagiarize a page from your repertoire and tell him that your dad has a bad back from the mill and cannot drive. My dad works in the foundry and does not know your dad. My dad is always ready to aid a damsel in distress."

Three miles outside of Ford City, Angelin declared, "I gotta go potty."

"Why did you not squeeze it out twenty minutes ago while we were still in Ford City?"

"I didn't have to go then."

"You could ask at a farmhouse to use the bathroom. But most of the houses here have outhouses, though."

"Yuckies… What would you do if you had to go?"

"I would randomly select any point along the road and walk twenty feet away from the road, and then I would whip it out."

"I gotta do the other kind, number two."

"We are too far from home to simply hold it."

"Oh no, the explosion is gonna be soon."

"At the bottom of the hill is a bridge over a crick. If I were you, I would walk down to the base of the bridge and do it there, where no one, except the cows, can see you."

We rode down to the bridge. Joanie looked over the edge. A car drove by. Joanie's eyes followed the car, expecting the occupants to sing, "We know where you're go'n, we know what you're do'n."

"I gotta go now. But how do you do it?"

I pointed to the gravel flat at the base of the arched bridge. "Stand there. Lean back as if you were going to sit in a chair and let your back press against the cement. Your back supports you even though you are not sitting on anything. Pull your pants down and dump." I walked to a tree and demonstrated the position by leaning back against it.

Angelin flared her lips and sucked in a deep breath as she peered pensively up the road and then glanced behind her. She scratched the back of her head and jokingly said, "You wouldn't happen to have a roll of TP, would'ja?" I walked back to the kitbag dangling from the handlebars of my bike. I drew a quarter-roll of toilet paper and tossed it, end over end, to Angelin. She cried in astonishment, "You carry TP with you?"

"Do you think I have never been on a long bike ride before?"

⁂

On Saturday morning of the autumnal equinox, Dad let Angelin drive his car to Ford City to take the driver's test. It was only the fourth time she had been behind the wheel. She was so cautious that she stopped at every intersection, even when she had the right of way. She used the turn signal when she went around a bend on the same road on which she was traveling. When we arrived at the testing center, Dad wanted to leave us with the car so that he could walk to the custard stand three blocks up the street. But I insisted that he enter the center and sit with us so that the troopers would see that an adult had accompanied us in the car. In the center, the bad news was—the Italian trooper was not there. Officer Mrasz was alone. The good news was—my dad was there. When Officer Mrasz said, "Next," I immediately sprang to my feet and approached his desk.

"Dzien dobry, Officer Mrasz. Jak sie masz?"

"The officer grinned and greeted with "Daniel, Dzien dobry."

"I would like you to meet my dad." Dad came to the desk. The two men shook hands and conversed in Polish.

"So, Daniel, you going to take the driver's test today?"

"No sir, my girlfriend, Angelin, is."

⁂

Poor Angelin—when she started the car, she held the key too long and grinded the starter flywheel. My dad grimaced as if the sound emanating from his mistress was vicariously driving a stake through his heart. I muttered, "It sounds horrible, but it is not a safety issue. Maybe she will garner some sympathy points." The driving part of the exam was a joke. Mrasz had Angelin drive only a three-block square around the center. Angelin drove only ten miles per hour. Maybe Mrasz was scared that he would never get back if he requested her to go farther. When they returned to the center, Mrasz told Angelin to pull up along the curb. Cautious Angelin parked two feet away from the curb. They sat in the car while Mrasz asked, "How far from a fire hydrant must you park?"

Angelin had no sense of distance. She thought thirty feet was a reasonable distance. So, to play it safe, she doubled the estimate and replied, "Sixty feet."

"Twenty feet would be sufficient," Mrasz said. "How do you apply the brakes when it's icy?"

"Well," Angelin replied, "you take it easy."

"You should pump the breaks when it's icy." Mrasz scribbled some notes on a form that was clamped onto a clipboard. "OK, Miss Bugliese, let's return to the office…………You passed."

Chapter XIV

"Allô, Daniel. C'est moi, Marie," Mary Jane called to me from the steps leading to the cellar in my house. My sister must have let Mary Jane in and directed her to Dad's workbench. "My mother's new boyfriend has a bunch of his friends visiting, so I decided to get scarce. What are you doing down here?"

"I will try to sharpen this blade on my mower."

"Whew, what happened to it?"

"At the end of the season, I hit a steel rod lurking in the weeds at old Caracelli's place. I do not know whether it is salvageable."

"So, this is what you decided to do on a snowy afternoon? I thought you would be out making an ungodly fortune shoveling snow."

"I shall, after the snow starts to slow down. No one wants to hire you while the snow is still falling. Besides, I need to see if this blade is beyond redemption. I might have to put in an order at the catalog distribution center, if I want it to arrive before spring mowing season."

Mary Jane hopped onto the stool on which my dad had me sit when giving me haircuts. "Do you know Tommy McCain?" she asked.

"Yea, he is a junior. He lives down somewhere in the streets named after trees."

"Is he a … popular guy at Kiski?" Mary Jane asked.

"Tommy? Yea. He is always smiling and slapping people on the back. He plays football. Rumor has it that he is a good slot back, whatever that is. How do you know Tommy McCain?"

"He asked me out."

"Son of a b…" I exhaled as the wrench slipped and stripped the edges of the bolt I was trying to loosen. That ended any hope of screwing the bolt off… I had never contemplated competition when it came to Joanie and Angelin. But I had always feared that guys would eventually discover the little beauty. "That pisses me off. Tommy should know that you are my girl."

"Why should he know when I do not even know it? Please explain the difference between being a girlfriend and being the girlfriend to you."

I did not reply immediately. I pretended to work while I desperately searched for an answer. "Look, I know that our arrangement is a tad unusual. But it works so well for us."

"For us?" Mary Jane laughed sarcastically. "No, Daniel, it works very well for *you*." Mary Jane pretended to look at the map of streams in Pennsylvania hanging on the wall. "Friends, no—not friends—classmates tell me, 'Mary Jane, we saw you out with Daniel on Friday night, then we saw him with some older girl last night.' A girlfriend should not have to put up with that. A real girlfriend would not put up with it."

"Angelin and Joanie have had similar experiences."

"Stop right there," Mary Jane blurted. "Do not compare me with them any more. I am sorry. They are my best friends, but I will not let that stop me from having normal expectations and a normal life. They accept les triplés because they have no choice. For them, it is you or being alone. Do not judge me using their standards. I am not unreasonable. If they were decent looking, they would have confronted you long ago about this … this arrangement. If I am the hottest property on the block, then I want an exclusive address. I am sorry. That probably sounded crass, but I need to be realistic. I need to be honest, especially with myself, about what I want."

I pulled the other stool to face Mary Jane. I slid onto it. "You have not been happy with me?"

"Happy is relative. I have been happy sometimes, but never satisfied. I am not my mother. She pleads for a commitment. I demand it."

"But I have always been committed to you. I have never dated anyone else other than … the three of you. I have never lied to you. And I promise that I will never leave you. Does that not count for something?"

"Those things count. That is way more than my mother ever got. But I want the whole enchilada."

"What did you tell him? I mean, you said 'no,' right?"

"Yea, I said 'no' … the first time." The cavern became eerily silent. The glow from the clear light bulb reflected in Mary Jane's eyes. She was so beautiful. "Tommy called last night and asked me again. I told him I needed to think about it."

I hated to hear Mary Jane say the word, Tommy. It sounded so personal, so intimate, too real. I had a vision of Tomm … him kissing her neck. A burning sensation crept into the back of my neck. A girl who means "no" says it more emphatically when asked a second time. When a boy is told *no* and subsequently hears "maybe" on the second pass, he is powerfully encouraged, encouraged more than if he had heard a non-committal *maybe* the first time. The second round *maybe* entails the big Momentum towards the direction of yes. "Tommy McCain, of all people, is not the right guy for you. You would not be happy with him."

"How would you know? It does not sound like you know him very well at all."

"Exactly the point," I said with the added emphasis of splaying the fingers of my right hand. "I have been in the same grade in the same schools with that guy since seventh grade, and I have never had a class with him. That should tell you something. I have taken classes at some time with everyone who possesses at least some degree of sentience. You are a brilliant girl. I can appreciate you. What is it about Tommy McCain that you like, anyway?"

"Well, he is really, really cute."

Damned, I wish she had not said that. I thought, {*If I am ever the one to end a relationship, I shall never talk-up the new girl in front of the jilted one.*} I stood up and paced around the workbench. "This is a nightmare. I cannot believe this is happening. I cannot believe that you are leaving me for the likes of Tommy McCain, of all people."

"I am not leaving you, Daniel. But you may be leaving me. Have you not been listening to me? I love you. I have loved you since the first time I served you iced tea when you came over to my house to pull weeds. I want to stay with you forever. That is all I have ever wanted. But it has to be an exclusive one-on-one. You will have to break up with Joanie and Angelin. It will have to be a clean break. You cannot hang out with them. With the exception of a few words during a chance encounter at school, you must not have contact with them, no having lunch together at school, no phone calls. I hate making such tough conditions. I will never ask you to restrict contacts with anyone else. I may even agree to ease the restrictions regarding Angelin and Joanie, but no time soon. It is because you love them and they love you that a dramatic change must happen. I know you, Daniel. Absent rules, you would say 'yes' to me and then make every effort to give the appearance to Joanie and Angelin that nothing had really changed and that the relationships should continue. Your tendency of saying 'Yes Mommy' and then doing whatever you please is not going to work with me. Well, enough said. It is decision time, my love—me or them."

I did not respond, not because of indecision, but rather because I had immediately known my decision and was paralyzed by thoughts of the consequences. I loved Angelin and Joanie, but I was in love with Mary Jane. I would have traded the world to keep Mary Jane. Since my decision was not at issue for me, the consequences haunted me with the thoughts of cruelty to be visited upon Joanie and Angelin. How was I to look into their eyes and reject them, to betray years of trust that I had fostered, to hurt them like they had never been hurt before, and to abandon them to loneliness? Mary Jane chose a gambit that would result in either having me exclusively or Tommy McCain, but not loneliness. There was no one in the wings to sweep Angelin or Joanie off her feet if I were to pull the plug. The thought of their suffering literally made me sick.

Seeing my distress, Mary Jane said, "Look, Daniel, I really blindsided you on this. I know that you are in agony. Take a few days, five days, to decide. I love you."

ॐॐॐ

Mary Jane's description of me being in agony was an understatement. A few days earlier, I had been a happy guy. I thought, {*But now, one way or the other, a vital part of the core of my being is about to be destroyed.*} I was trim before Mary Jane dropped the bomb. Over five days, my pants became baggy from lack of eating. I was gaunt. Joanie, Angelin, my family, classmates, teachers, clients—everyone could see that I was distressed. I made two unsuccessful attempts to get Mary Jane to rescind the ultimatum. When with Angelin and Joanie, I was attentive and sweet to them, partly out of a sense of guilt. I savored the moments as if they were flashbacks of a less complicated, carefree and happier time. Oddly, the only time I ate was late night of day four. Under emotional exhaustion that evening, I daydreamed of refusing to make a decision. The thought gave me a respite. I whispered, "I could stand being in the same room with myself. No one would be devastated, except for me. Joanie and Angelin would not be hurt. Mary Jane gets to choose an option with which she is most comfortable. And I shall lose the love of my life."

Mary Jane came to my house after school on Thursday to hear my decision. I made another plea to put a stop to the destruction. Actually, she had considered many times removing the ultimatum. But she did not give me a hint of her ambivalence. She had ended all of the debates with herself, resolved that she could not continue without a change. "Bottom line," I concluded, "I am so in love with you that I cannot lose you." Mary Jane offered to go with me to Joanie's house where Angelin and Joanie were baking braided sweet challah breads. I insisted that Mary Jane not go but accepted that she walk me there, but not go in.

It was a crystal clear day. The sun blinded me as we walked in its direction. I had walked the route a thousand times before, yet I could not remember the sun ever having been in my eyes before. In the glare, the image developed of Joanie and Angelin as little girls picking up rocks in the brook to help me build the dam. I shuddered. The glare made the route look unfamiliar. I just wanted to go home and to crawl up in bed. My heart pounded, and I felt a dull headache. The sun was unrelenting. Bathed in light, I could not see. I tripped over a frost heave in the walkway. Stumbling to regain my footing, a wave of nausea rolled through me, followed by a hot flash and sweats. The sun was suffocating me. My trembling knees buckled. I was sitting on the curb, but I did not know how I got there.

"You cannot stop now," Mary Jane pleaded. "You are ready to choose us to be together. The house is right there. You can do it. Come on. I will help you up." Mary Jane scooped my arm and tugged to get me to stand up.

"No, it is no use. Please stop, Mary Jane. I cannot do it. It is no longer a matter of choice. I cannot abandon them."

"No-o-o!" Mary Jane cried. When she released my arm, Mary Jane stumbled backwards. She reeled around to face Joanie's house. Gulping two gasps, she started running towards the house. I stumbled to my feet and ran after her. Mary Jane ran through the front entrance, through the parlor and into the kitchen, with me following. Joanie and Angelin were startled by the raucous entrance. None of us had ever entered Joanie's house without knocking. We had always gone to the kitchen door, never through the front door like Mary Jane did.

Our obviously desperate visage prompted Angelin to ask, "What's wrong?"

Mary Jane drew in a breath and announced, "Daniel has decided to have me as his one and only girlfriend. We love each other. I … we are very sorry to hurt each of you. But Daniel will not be dating nor seeing either of you anymore. It is over. We are very sorry."

The surreal nightmare revisited a hundred times during the week was reenacted, but not as I had imagined. Angelin was uncharacteristically silent. She slowly turned and stared out the window. She, along with Joanie and Mary Jane, knew that les triplés was an unrealistic arrangement. Only Daniel was naïve enough to hope that it could hold. Angelin had known for years that pretty Mary Jane would someday make a demand that Daniel could not refuse. She wondered why it took Mary Jane so long. Angelin faced the inevitability with existential resignation and with dignity.

"Is it true, Daniel?" Joanie choked. "Are you leaving me?" I could not speak. I could not even look at Joanie. I was a coward. How I detested myself. Joanie slid around the kitchen table and clutched my arms. "Tell me, Daniel," Joanie sobbed. "Is it … Look at me!" She cried, clutching and shaking my sweatshirt at chest level. The corner of my right upper eyelid twitched as I looked up at Joanie. "Are you leaving me?" she whimpered.

I swallowed and said, "No, I am not leaving you. I never will leave you." Joanie collapsed while still holding onto my sweatshirt. I instinctively dropped with her, placing my hand on her back to prevent her head from hitting the floor. Angelin's head twisted around in utter amazement. My response shocked her more than Mary Jane's announcement. Mary Jane's eyes, face and body drooped as she slowly turned and walked out of the house.

"Mary Jane," I called as I sprang to my feet and followed her. "Mary Jane, stop, will ya?" She threw a hand out to her side, indicating that I was to leave her alone and to not follow. "Mary Jane, it cannot end this way!" Her pace slowed to a stop. She lowered her head and made two fists. She turned and walked determinedly towards me, but averted her eyes. Throwing her arms around me, Mary Jane's soft lips kissed me passionately. The love of my life turned and walked away.

Chapter XV

I lost my balance, oscillating between lethargy and maniacal absorption into jobs, the more exhausting—the better. School diminished in significance. I blew off a week of math classes covering the techniques for using the slide rule. Joanie was upset with me for missing the slipstick demonstrations. She chided, "The slide rule is a skill that you will probably need throughout your life."

I swung between treating Angelin and Joanie badly and trying to recompense by acting overly sweetly to them. But no amount of niceness could compensate for treating them badly. I could not understand why I directed my anger against the girls. Did I believe that they were at fault—as if it so happened that Joanie and Angelin had not existed, then I would still have my precious Mary Jane? Sometimes I blamed Mary Jane. Were her interests important enough to justify this much damage? Mostly, though, I blamed myself for not having the fortitude to do what it would have taken to keep Mary Jane.

I changed into a different person. I acted like a mouse in a house with special routes designed to avoid being detected. When I left my house, I always used the back door and continued walking straight through the backyard, from which I entered the alley. To catch the school bus, I walked the alley for three blocks and turned down on Wallace Street. The route was circuitous and inefficient. I hated inefficiency. Yet, I did it just to avoid Mary Jane because I just could not handle seeing her. After each class at the high school, I made a beeline for the nearest exit to the fields surrounding Kiski High. I walked the fields way out of my way and reentered the high school at the sophomore hallway. I went through that process to avoid contact with Tommy McCain in my building, the junior building. I did not blame

Tommy for the catastrophe. He did what one would expect a guy to do. If Tommy had not asked out Mary Jane, another guy would have. I was hiding from a kid whom I really did not know. I never had hidden from anyone in my life. I was even developing contingency plans to avoid running into Mary Jane in the fall when she was to start at Kiski. I considered transferring to Mum's stupid prep school.

A week after the meltdown in Joanie's kitchen, I resolved to see Mary Jane, to work things out between us so we could get back together. While on the side walkway leading from my back porch, I spotted Mary Jane emerging from her house. Tommy was with her. I darted behind a rhododendron. Mary Jane and Tommy were followed by her mother's boyfriend. Old beer-gut acted as if Tommy was his new best friend. Ear-bush must have been super-impressed because Tommy was a football player. God, how I hated football. Tommy opened the passenger door to his father's car. Mary Jane looked so cute getting into the car. Tommy smiled at her as he closed the door. His act of capture and possession of … my girl … made me seethe. I bolted up the walkway, past my back porch and through my backyard. I ran full throttle up the alley and turned onto Hancock Avenue. I sprinted the entire half-mile hill, up Hancock Avenue. At the summit, I collapsed against a rock near the town's water tank. My temples palpitated. A much welcomed numbness permeated my body as large, wet snowflakes alighted on my face.

⚝⚝⚝

When Tommy got into the car, he asked Mary Jane for some money. "I've already blown my allowance," Tommy explained. "And we need to get gas." The request surprised Mary Jane. She did not get an allowance, and Daniel surely had not. Whenever les triplés had needed to fund an activity, Daniel had covertly slipped Mary Jane some money. When it had been time to ante up, she had produced her share, giving the appearance of shared support. Mary Jane gave Tommy three dollars out of her emergency stash.

After cleaning the windshield, the service station attendant asked if Tommy wanted him to check the oil level. "Yes, please," Tommy replied. "I've been burning oil. Usually, I need to add a quart every time I gas up."

They watched Tommy's favorite nephew play the second half of a junior high basketball game. Tommy referred to his nephew as "the kid," which amused Mary Jane because the nephew was only a year younger than she. On the way home, Tommy took a long way that led to the lane on which one of his uncles lived. His uncle was on a trip, so the lane was deserted. Mary Jane was not opposed to making out as long as it did not go too far. As he worked his hand up her thigh, she thought, {W*hy did I not wear culottes?*} She did not know when to say no. Part of her argued the domino theory—if I do not stop it here and now, then where and when? Mary Jane did not know what to do, so she invoked the female default rule—if in doubt, just say no. Mary Jane's forceful demeanor barely controlled his raging hormones. Tommy exercised restraint because he knew he was on probation. Although Mary Jane tactfully did not talk about Daniel, Tommy had heard enough rumors to know that Daniel remained a rival.

ॐॐॐ

Before going to a McCain family picnic, Tommy had a special favor to do for his mother. He drove Mary Jane down an alley in the old part of Leechburg. They stopped by a brick building that was a defunct Croatian club. Tommy led Mary Jane through the building's coal bin entrance into a basement set up with three poker tables and a roulette wheel. "I do not think we should be here," Mary Jane said.

"We're not going to be here long. We're just going to pick up Uncle Pete. And if he's plastered, it might take the both of us to do it."

Uncle Pete was at the roulette wheel. Tommy's Aunt Jen was beside Uncle Pete, pleading, "For the love of the Mother of Jesus, Pete, your paycheck is almost gone. Please leave this place now."

Uncle Pete made a gesture with the back of his hand, feigning a strike at his wife. His beet-red face sprayed saliva as he growled back at his wife, "Leave me alone. I'm on the verge of winning big. I'm working hard here, can't you see? I'm working hard, and it's all for you, all for you. I'm gonna make it up to you, Jen. You'll see. I'm on the verge of winning. I'm gonna be a winner. I've been faithfully placing my money on number 32 all afternoon. All of the other numbers have hit over and over again. Number seventeen has hit nine times already. Nine times, I've been counting. But number 32 has never hit. So, don't you see?"

"See what, Pete?" Aunt Jen cried.

"It's due, 32 is due. By the Law of Averages, it's bound to hit anytime now."

Tommy cautiously approached his uncle and said, "Hey, Uncle Pete, your big sister says it's time to go." Tommy laid a hand on Uncle Pete's arm. Uncle Pete reflexively threw his arm back to break Tommy's hold.

"Get off of me! How dare you? Do you want me to lose? I can't lose," Uncle Pete whispered, "because I have a system. I worked hard on this." Uncle Pete pulled out a pocket note pad with all of the roulette numbers on it with slash marks beside the numbers corresponding to the frequency of each number hitting. "I've kept a tally of every hit. Number 32 is due. The Law of Averages guarantees it. The difference between a winner and a loser is that a loser walks away just before his number is called. A winner hangs in there tough. Thirty-two could be the next number or maybe the one after. It's due. I've kept track."

Mary Jane watched the steel ball glide around the wheel. As the ball dropped into a slot, its selection process appeared to be random. Again and again, Mary Jane observed the randomness of the ball falling into a slot. Mary Jane tugged on Tommy's shirt sleeve and said, "Come on, get your uncle, and let us get the hell out of here."

Tommy replied, "But look at his crib sheet. Number 32 really is due."

"But Tommy, watch the roulette. The number selection is random."

"Yea, so what?"

Mary Jane watched the ball going around at that very moment and said, "If the selection right now is random, then there is no causal connection between this roll and all of the prior rolls. That ball has an equal probability of hitting number seventeen again as it has of hitting number thirty-two or any other number, regardless of history."

"But what about the Law of Averages?" Tommy queried.

Uncle Pete suddenly vomited a gruel of highballs and peanuts. The owner of the parlor was more than glad to assist us in dragging Uncle Pete out into the alley.

⊰⊰⊰

Mary Jane walked the half-mile downhill to Tommy's house where he was playing pitcher in a game of kickball with the kids. Tommy enjoyed playing with his eight-year-old brother, two nephews and a niece. When she arrived at Tommy's backyard, Mary Jane sat on the above-ground edge of one of the two angled walls that formed the entrance for the short, outside stairwell to the cellar. Tommy smiled at Mary Jane as he pitch-rolled an inflated ball towards his niece. The children were having a lot of fun. Tommy was a natural with kids, a trait of which Mary Jane took special notice. She did not have a father and no father figure in her life … well, except maybe, to some extent, Daniel. Tommy's natural rapport with children made him more attractive to Mary Jane. She thought, {*Maybe I will let him go …a little further next time.*} For the first time since the break up, Mary Jane was not thinking of Daniel.

Uncle Ted slipped Tommy a dollar bill with which to buy penny candy for the children. Tommy, Mary Jane and the kids walked the six blocks to the five-and-ten on the main business street. One of the nephews, named Skip, repeatedly looked at Mary Jane and said, "Yer beautiful. Will you marry me?" At the store and close to the glass encasement of the candy was a kite display. Two assembled kites, with images of rockets on the paper sheath, hung from a pillar. A sign posted the price of nineteen cents. The children's eyes lit up at the sight of the kites. Skip boisterously proclaimed, "Let's buy kites."

"Sorry guys," Tommy said. "We don't have enough money. Check out the penny candy."

Mary Jane tugged at Tommy's sleeve and whispered, "But you have a dollar."

"Yea? So?"

Mary Jane looked back at the price sign and said, "All four could get kites for only seventy-six cents. You would still have a little money left over for some candy."

"The kites would only cost seventy-six cents? How do you know that?" he asked with eyes furrowed.

"Seriously? … Well, nineteen is close to twenty, so I multiplied twenty times four kids, to get eighty. I took the one cent difference between twenty and nineteen and multiplied the one cent difference times four kites and subtracted the four cents from eighty to get seventy-six."

"Is that what they teach in those classes for nerds?"

Mary Jane giggled. But when Tommy appeared insulted, her grin immediately melted from her face. She never intended to offend. She just thought that Tommy was making a joke. "No, the school does not teach that technique."

"Well, how can you figure that out so fast?"

"I … I … just do it… When multiplying, I set a benchmark within a reasonable range. Then I adjust from the benchmark to get the answer."

"Well, whatever," Tommy said as if Mary Jane had spoken a foreign language. He turned to the children and gleefully cried, "Everyone picks a kite."

Mary Jane swallowed.

Chapter XVI

On an unseasonably warm day in late March, Angelin and I waited for Joanie to join us to go to lunch. I sat on a stone slab that was part of the base of a sculpture made of twisted and soldered rusting metal. Angelin was standing with one foot resting atop a stone slab. My back was to the sculpture, but Angelin rested her elbows upon a knee and intently examined the sculpture. Angelin said, "I've passed this monstrosity a thousand times. I'm about to graduate, and I have never closely looked at it. What do you think of it?"

Without turning around I replied, "I think the school district ran out of money, so they went to a junkyard and randomly picked up some scrap pieces and had the guys from the metal shop class weld them together."

Fedge Hirranacan, a classmate from Angelin's senior class, walked by us. His real name was John, but everyone called him Fedge. "Fedge, what do you think of our objet d'art?" Angelin queried.

Fedge shrugged and said, "I don't care enough about it to have an opinion."

"What?" Angelin mocked indignation. "You do not treasure Appalachian art?"

Fedge stopped momentarily. He rolled his eyes at the sculpture and explained, "If you can't eat it, if you can't drink it, and if you can't smoke it or screw it, then what good is it?"

As Fedge walked away, Angelin sat beside me and said, "There goes a guy with an uncomplicated value system." In the distance, we could see Joanie coming. Angelin and I stood and walked to rendezvous with Joanie at the cafeteria doorway.

Over a lunch of spaghetti with a watery sauce and gristly ground meat, I proposed a fabulously lucrative profit-making endeavor. I pulled out a dollar bill and requested the girls read its obverse. It read, "This certifies that there is on deposit in the Treasury of the United States of America one dollar in silver payable to the bearer on demand."

"This is a silver certificate," I said. "If you have 129 of these, the U.S. Treasury will exchange them for a one-hundred ounce bar of pure silver. So, the Treasury's exchange rate is $1.29 per ounce. The world price for silver is three dollars. So, if you can buy an ounce for only $1.29 if you have these, what do you think that does to the value of these?" I held up the silver certificate.

"You want to buy bars of silver from the U.S Treasury?" Joanie tried to clarify.

"No. I do not even know where the U.S. Treasury is located, other than Washington, D.C. Instead, coin dealers are buying the certificates and selling them to even bigger dealers who eventually do trade them for huge amounts of silver. Right now, dealers in Pittsburgh are paying a dollar and a quarter for a certificate, which is way below its true value."

Joanie opened her purse and dug out three dollar bills. Scrutinizing them, she cried with an adrenaline rush, "I've got one! I've got one! Can I get a dollar and a quarter for it?"

"You will get a lot more for it than that as the deadline approaches for redeeming them."

"What deadline?" Both girls demanded.

"The gravy train could not last forever. The Treasury has stopped making the certificates and has set a deadline for redemption sometime in June. As the deadline approaches the dealers will become frenzied in their pursuit of this bonanza. As the deadline nears, they will pay more and more and will pay a premium if you have a big stack."

"What's a big stack?" Joanie blurted. I knew I would not have trouble getting her involved.

"Well, unfortunately, our limit is going to be in the hundreds," I replied.

"What?" Joanie exhaled. "Where are we gonna get hundreds of dollars?"

I shrugged and replied, "I have four hundred dollars in savings with which I planned to buy stock this month. I am delaying the stock purchase to devote the money towards this project for the next two months. I might be able to borrow a few more bucks from my dad, if I have him hold as collateral the certificates we collect in the next few weeks."

Joanie gasped, "You accumulated four hundred dollars from those piddly jobs you work?"

Angelin grunted, "Remember, he never spends a dime of it … on himself. But how do we get hundreds of theses certificates?"

"First, notice how easy they are to identify. The silver certificate has a small blue seal on the front. No other dollar bill has that blue seal. You can quickly shuffle through a stack of dollar bills and find the certificates in them. Now,… we have the lower bank and the upper bank on Grant Street. I go to the lower bank and withdraw all of the money from my savings account. I will request payment in one-dollar bills only."

"You sound like a bank robber," Joanie giggled.

"They do not care," I said. "The bank has plenty of ones. I pull out the silver certificates. I add in the dollars my dad lends me. I go to the upper bank and trade the dollars in for coin rolls."

"How much in coins will the bank give you?"

"Maybe a couple hundred dollars worth, if I have a good reason, like the Kiski Area Polio Children's Benefit Bake Sale."

"You're really bad," Angelin chided and laughed at the same time.

"Then I give the coins to Joanie, and she goes to the upper bank and trades them for one dollar bills. After we remove the silver certificates, Joanie then goes to the lower bank and trades the dollars for coins. And then, it is Angelin's turn."

"The banks are going to figure out what we're doing," Joanie cautioned.

"I am not so sure. We will keep a log of which tellers we use. If we keep a diversified rotation of tellers, they may not become wise to us. Besides, we are not permanently draining one particular denomination of currency out of either bank. We take dollars out, we put dollars back in. We take coins out, and we put them back in. The only thing that is permanent is the winnowing of silver certificates. But just in case the banks get wise, we need an alternative plan. I will give each of you twenty one-dollar Federal Reserve Notes. Observe that everyone you see has dollar bills in his wallet or her purse. You just have to ask them to let you look at their ones. When you spot a silver certificate, ask to make the trade." I looked around the room for a person to ask to see his dollar bills. "Joanie, go ask Flyman to let you see his dollars." I nodded slightly to the left where Flyman sat at the end of our row of tables.

"Oooh, he's so creepy. Why are you asking ME to go?"

"Because he is hot for you."

"Gee thanks for the compliment." Joanie glanced at Flyman out of the corner of an eye. "Why's he called Flyman? Does he want to join the Air Force?"

"No-o-o," Angelin replied. "When I was in ninth grade and you were in eighth, the cafeteria in dear old Vandergrift Junior High was closed for a week. Remember when we had to bring our own lunches and eat them in the gym? We were able to buy milk at a booth. One day, Flyman had bought his milk and was sitting at a table with his food unwrapped. He was ready to eat when he discovered that he'd forgotten a straw for his milk. He got up and went to the milk booth to get a straw. Meanwhile, Gus Kasoulis found a dead fly. Gus lifted the bread on Flyman's sandwich and dropped the fly into it. About fifty people in the gym knew that the fly was in the sandwich and watched intently while Flyman ate every last piece of the sandwich. Henceforth, the name …"

"Stop, stop, you're going to make me sick," Joanie pleaded.

"Come on, girl, you can't be squeamish when you eat in the cafeteria. Who knows what's going on in the food prep room. Those guys are such pranksters. We've all probably eaten flies and maybe a cockroach or two, along with kah-kah from under their nails, boogers, spit and sperm."

Joanie glared at her cold spaghetti, with its ground mystery meat, and whimpered, "I'm going on a diet."

ॐॐॐ

On Saturday, May 19, I took a six A.M. bus to Pittsburgh, carrying my dad's old, black, scuffed-up lunchbox. Inside were envelopes containing fifty silver certificates in each, 437 certificates in total. It was almost three weeks from the Treasury's deadline for redeeming silver certificates. I dared not risk waiting any longer. I went to the meeting rooms at the Forbes Hotel, which hosted a coin show with many dealers. I circulated from dealer to dealer, dickering price. After negotiating with every dealer, I repeated the circuit. The dealers hated my process of creating a bidding war that carved deeply into their profit margins. All the same, when the dealers realized that I was negotiating with all of them, they grudgingly raised their bids seriously closely to their true cut-off point. I sold at $1.61 on face.

Chapter XVII

"Hello, Mrs. McCain, Mary Jane here. Is Tommy in?"

"Hello, Mary Jane. I think Tommy's in the garage lifting weights… Jerry, tell your brother out in the garage that Mary Jane's on the line." As she waited, Mary Jane checked her face in the mirror. Since last night, Mary Jane had noticed an unfamiliar soreness deep underneath the surface of the skin on her face.

"Hi Snuggly Bear."

"Tommy, I appreciate the showing of endearment in your choice of a nickname for me. But do you really have to call me Snuggly Bear?"

"Whad'ya want me to call you?"

"How about Mary Jane?"

"But everyone has a nickname, especially girlfriends."

"OK, then how about something more dynamic, like … Electra?"

"What kind of name is that?"

"Electra was a young woman in ancient Greek mythology."

"Oh."

"The reason I called, Tommy, is because I have noticed that you tend to quickly fill your, or should I say *our*, weekend schedule pretty early in the week. So, I thought that I could make a preemptive suggestion before you get us all booked up for this weekend. I am looking at the Vandergrift paper as I speak and see that the Casino will be showing a remake of the movie, *Rebecca*. I thought we could see it on Saturday, perhaps a matinee."

"Well, what's it about?"

"A young, shy English girl is a—what would one call it—a paid companion to a cranky old woman. They travel on holiday to Italy where the young girl meets and falls in love with a filthy rich Englishman twice her age. He is a widower with a dark past…"

"Whoa, whoa. You sure sound like you know a lot about the movie. Did you already see it?"

"No, but I read the book by Daphne du Maurier." Actually, most of the book had been read aloud to Mary Jane. "The book was great, and if the movie is half as g…"

"Is there much action in the movie? It don't sound like it."

"I do not think it would be classified as an action movie. It is more like a mystery and, of course, a romance." Mary Jane's voice rose with excitement when she added, "There are moments of suspense, yea, a lot of suspense."

"Hey, you know, that sounds really great. But a bunch of guys on the team are thinking of having a party at Stitt's Bluff on Saturday. I would like to take you to meet them. The left guard—his name is Pooza—he saw you with me last week. He says that you are one fine-looking babe. You know what he told me? He said that he'd eat a mile of your shit just to see where it came from. Ole Pooza, the guy's a barrel of laughs. You'll just love'm."

"Will there be any booze at the party?"

"Oh, well, probably some. It's OK. You'll see. You'll have a great time."

"But what if the cops show up?"

"Oh hell, that's no problem. Most of the cops were on the team years ago. We just go over to them and start shoot'n the bull about the good ole days. We snow them by telling'm that if we were half as good as they were, we'd be goin to the state championship game.… Hey, how about this? Why don't we go to the party, and then we'll look at the flicks next week? Whad'ya say? Oh, please, please, Snuggly Bear."

ა៖ა៖ა៖

On the way to the party at Stitt's Bluff, Tommy and Mary Jane drove along River Road to Giuseppe's Restaurant to collect eight pizzas that were pre-ordered. They entered on the bar side of the building. While Tommy transacted business with Giuseppe, Mary Jane ambled to a hardwood, standing shuffleboard on which a player slides heavy, stainless steel pucks over a fine grit sprinkled across the playing surface of the shuffleboard. Mary Jane picked up a puck and slid the fingers of her free hand across it. She was intrigued by its compact weight and smoothness. Taking position on the other end of the shuffleboard, Tommy picked up a puck and forcefully flung it along the playing board towards Mary Jane, where it banged into the holding trough on her end. The bang startled Mary Jane, who had not been paying attention to it. Tommy grasped another puck and commanded, "Defend thyself."

"Get the puck off of me," Mary Jane replied as she placed her puck near the end of the board. She held a hand atop the puck to maneuver it as a defender against Tommy's impudent assaults. After defending against a few shots, Mary Jane began to anticipate his throws and to fling her pucks to intercept his at mid-board. Mary Jane and Tommy giggled as they jousted to knock each other's puck from the field of combat.

When Giuseppe emerged from the kitchen through the double swinging doors, he cried, "Hey you kids, stop that roughhousing. That's not a toy. Get away from the shuffleboard."

Tommy picked up five pizza boxes, and Mary Jane picked up the remaining three. After distributing the boxes across the back seat of his car, Tommy reached into his jacket and revealed a puck. An astonished Mary Jane asked, "What are you going to do with that?" Tommy shrugged and tendered the puck towards Mary Jane as a gift. She flinched a half-step backwards, grimaced and said, "I do not want it."

Tommy grinned and shrugged with indifference. After taking three steps back from the car, he placed the puck into the palm of his right hand. Crouching like a discus thrower and spinning in a circle twice, Tommy flung the puck with all of his might. A distinctly solid plopping sound emanated from mid-pool of the Kiskiminetas River.

ॐॐॐ

"OK, so what is going on here?" I demanded.

"Nothing," Joanie said with a fake smile.

"Bullshit. You two were cackling away like two magpies until I approached. So, what is the secret?"

"Oh, just girl talk."

I looked at Joanie who looked flustered. Angelin averted eye contact with me. Fortunately for me, neither was a good liar. "This is the last time I am going to ask. What are you concealing?"

"We would be violating a promise," Joanie pleaded. I grabbed and twisted her left ear which caused her to collapse onto the chair beside her. "OK, OK! Let me go. I went to see Mary Jane this morning."

I released Joanie and said, "Oh? Well, good. How is she?"

"OK, except she has that intestinal virus that's going around."

"What did you talk about?"

"Oh, stuff."

"Stuff?… Why did you decide to go see her after all this time?"

Joanie stared at Angelin. When I twisted around to see Angelin, she started to inspect Joanie's kitchen ceiling. Joanie stammered, "I … ah, I…"

"Do I have to twist your ears, again? Why are you putting me through this? Am I not always straight with you?"

"Look who's talking," Angelin piped in. "You would never violate a confidence."

"You would not be violating a confidence by telling me why you went to see Mary Jane."

Joanie shrugged and said, "I saw Tommy McCain walking Felicia Cisnicki from the chorus room."

I pooh-poohed the implication, "That does not necessarily mean anything."

"Felicia Cisnicki? She's never been just a friend to any guy. With her, it's hot girlfriend or nothing. Besides, she was holding his arm."

"When did you see this?"

Joanie stammered again, "Ah … well … like Tuesday."

I pushed off from the refrigerator against which I had been leaning. I double stiff-armed the kitchen table right beside where Joanie was sitting. "Tuesday? And you are just telling me now? We both glanced at Angelin. "And when did you know?"

"Je suis désolée, monsieur. Mais je ne parle pas Anglais," Angelin replied.

"I did not think Mary Jane would stay long with a nothing like Tommy McCain," I sniffed.

"Ah, Mary Jane didn't leave Tommy."

"Are you saying that Mary Jane does not know about Felicia Cisnicki?" I asked.

"Yea, she knows," Joanie replied.

"What are you saying—that Tommy dumped Mary Jane? No way. She is ten times better looking than he and a million times smarter. Felicia Cisnicki is hot, but she is not in Mary Jane's league." Behind my back, Angelin made a gesture for Joanie to see. Angelin placed two fingers on her tongue to imitate gagging.

"Daniel, Mary Jane has some affliction that has made her face and neck, and possibly elsewhere, a swath of hideous sores. She has not been out of her room for weeks. I've never seen her so down. She's depressed."

I bolted for the door and ran the whole way to Mary Jane's house.

ชนชนช

"Mom?!!" Mary Jane cried from her bed. "I cannot believe that she let anyone in here, especially you."

"Your mum is worried about you," I said. "You need your friends. I want to help."

"Go away, Daniel."

"Will you take that sheet off your head?"

"Are you crazy? You are the last person in the world I would let see me. I would not even let myself be seen in the streets of Calcutta. Besides, on top of the main event, I also have the stomach flu that is really contagious. You must go, Daniel."

"That's OK. I have already had that stomach flu a couple of days ago." I lied.

"Joanie promised she would not tell you."

"I tortured her, but she still would not talk. So, I injected her with sodium pentothal… How long will you have the lesions?"

"The doctors are not sure, possibly indefinitely," Mary Jane monotoned stoically.

"And school, how are you handling school?"

"My mom fed them a story. For a little while the school bought it and sent assignments home. Now, they are about to fail me for the year."

"You cannot let that happen. If you miss a year, it would seem like forever to get out of here."

"Here, in this room, is where I intend to spend the rest of my life."

"How is this for a deal? What do you say if I promised to walk you to school every day?"

"… That is ridiculous. You would miss the bus to Kiski."

"I will ride the bike to Kiski."

"You are not allowed to have a bike at the high school."

"I will hide it in the weeds by the entrance."

"What if it rains?"

"Then it rains. I have ridden in the rain plenty of times. Riding the Serpentine Road in the rain is a diverse riding experience."

"You expect me to expose myself to the world looking like this?" Mary Jane pulled the sheet from her head.

"Do you really give a damned what anyone else thinks?"

"There is only one person for whom I give a damned. So, what do you think of it, my face?"

I told Mary Jane the truth, which was the impression I had in my mind at that very moment. "You have the most beautiful eyes I have ever seen."

I noticed a library book on the bureau beside Mary Jane's bed. I picked up <u>Rebecca</u> by Daphne du Maurier. I opened to a random page. The first two words I saw were *Mrs. Danvers*. I smiled and shook my head. "Mrs. Danvers, that lady was a trip." I closed the book and reopened to the first page. Sitting at the end of the bed, I started reading aloud.

Chapter XVIII

"When did Daniel say he would meet us?" Angelin asked as she and Mary Jane again glanced out of the parlor window in Mary Jane's house.

"Five minutes. But I saw his father's mother go in. After Daniel showers, he will have to spend some obligatory time with Babci."

"Now there's a woman you'd never want to mess with. Daniel's father spends more time down at Babci's house than he does at his own. He does everything Babci says. And that drives Daniel's mom crazy, literally."

The conversation stopped. The silence made both girls feel uncomfortable. They had never before spent more than a few seconds together with just them alone. Angelin impatiently looked again out the window towards Daniel's house.

"I need to know," Mary Jane said. "What did you think when I made the play for Daniel?"

Angelin stared straight ahead. She cocked her head as she slowly twisted it towards Mary Jane sitting next to her on the sofa. "Are you sure you really want to go there?… OK, in summary I thought, 'Greedy Bitch.'"

"That is what I thought you thought."

"Was it worth it?"

"In a way it was," Mary Jane said. "Today, I am calmer, happier and more satisfied than I have ever been in my life. By taking the plunge, I never will have to wonder what it is like out there. I learned that there is no perfect situation and no perfect person. You have to identify what is most important to you and not dwell on the minor stuff. I wanted the total commitment from the perfect lover. After sharing Tommy with his cousins, nephews and the football team, I actually saw less of him than I had of Daniel. I became an addition to Tommy's collection of people. I traded you for Pooza."

"Thank you, my dear, you've always known how to brighten my day."

"It was exciting at the beginning. I wanted it to work. I focused myopically on the good stuff, and there are a lot of good things about Tommy. He is energetic, fun loving and a friend to a lot of people. He is loyal and involved with a gigantic extended family. Everyone wants to be around Tommy. As long as we were frenetically active, I could block the fact that we had nothing in common. My attraction for Tommy ended in the snap of the fingers, that fast. At one moment I could not wait for him to embrace me and touch me. Then, all of a sudden, as I realized just how dumb he truly was and that he was not the one, then snap—I did not want him to touch me anymore. I felt sorry for leading him on. But it was not my fault. I did not start dating him knowing that we were so incompatible… At any rate, I am sorry for all of the heartache I caused."

"Enough already with the mea culpa. Hey, if I looked half as good as you looked, I would have delivered Daniel an ultimatum. But I wouldn't have gone for Tommy McCain. Girl, what were you thinking?"

"Come on. I did not choose him. Girls do not choose guys. He chose me. He was the one who asked *me* out. I did not know him. Give me a break for crying out loud. He was cute, really really cute."

"So are the manikins at Hegelmeiers, but I wouldn't date them even though they have a higher IQ."

"Oh God, you are right. You know what the football players talk about in the huddle? Plays called by the coach are delivered to them using a three digit code. One number tells the fat guys up front, like Pooza, which way to lean to take up space. The second number tells the guys who catch the ball which routes to run. And the third number tells the running backs which ways to go. Tommy kept screwing up. So, the coach had the quarterback tell Tommy in the huddle which way to run. That worked great until the game when Scott, the first string quarterback, got knocked out of the game. The second string quarterback did not know where Tommy was supposed to run. So, Tommy had to make his best guess as to which way to go. On one play, everyone, including Tommy carrying the ball, was supposed to sweep to the right. The other team's defense was also anticipating a sweep to the right because our fat guys up front were unconsciously signaling the sweep by the way they were leaning before the ball was snapped. When the ball was snapped, everyone on our team and everyone on the other team's defense moved to the right. Everyone moved right, except Tommy who mistakenly guessed left. But no other player from either team was on the left side of the field. Tommy had a clear field through which to run for an eighty-yard touchdown. Afterwards, guys from the newspaper and the radio congratulated the coach for his brilliant play-calling."

"Ah, there's Daniel," Angelin reported. "Oh, oh, wait a minute. No, he's being called back in. He almost made it, but false alarm." Turning back to Mary Jane, Angelin asked, "What's it like partying with the football team?"

"Most are nice guys, like Tommy. Some are crude. Some are scary."

"Scary? How do you mean?"

"Those guys have been intoxicated by the cheer of the crowds every Friday night. They walk with a swagger. With cafeteria workers sneaking them free ice cream, and with the coach fixing problems and the cops looking the other way when they are drinking and acting rowdy, some believe that rules do not apply to them. They are used to getting what they want when they want it without consequences. When they graduate, and society gives them a broom or shovel, I do not think some of them will accept the diminished role. Add in all of that strength and testosterone, and you have a scary condition."

"You describe a world that is unknown to me," Angelin noted. "There is something, though, about your experiences that doesn't compute. You say that you knew that Tommy was not the one. Yet, I saw you right after Tommy dumped you. You were devastated."

"That was weird. I knew way before the end that we did not have a future. I had already started to pull away from him. When Tommy stopped calling, I should have been relieved. But I was crushed by the feeling of being jilted. I had never felt so alone. It was like the title to a mad-scientist type of science-fiction movie." Mary Jane made a megaphone out of her cupped hands and projected, "I WAS REJECT-ED BY A MORON!!"

Angelin burst out laughing. She said, "But you seem to have recovered from the trauma of rejection."

"Oh yeah, I am a lot happier today. Someday, but not soon, I will tell Daniel that his les triplés really is not that bad. Actually, it works fairly well. The problem I had was cultural. After being fed massive doses of Romeo & Juliet, Lancelot & Guinevere, Anna Karenina & Vronsky—we are brainwashed into thinking that happiness can be realized only in a one-on-one relationship."

The conversation paused as the girls peered out the window at Daniel's house. "Maybe we should go over there and rescue him," Angelin murmured.

"You know, one thing that I do not like about this summer is not being able to hang out with you and Daniel on weekdays while you are taking college classes. Sometime this week, do you think I could go with you to IUP and check out the place?"

Angelin knew that her opinion concerning Mary Jane's request was irrelevant. Ever since the reunification, Daniel was ultra sensitive about making Mary Jane feel welcome back into les triplés. Everyone was also concerned about the fragility of Mary Jane's psychological state while she grappled with the devastation to her face. Angelin said, "The campus is interesting. While Daniel and I are in class, you can tour the student union and the gym. You can use my I.D. to go swimming if you like. IUP has a great pool. The library has plays recorded on LP's. Record players with headphones are available for your use."

"Thanks, but I was hoping that I could go with you and Daniel to see what a college class is like. I would like to sit with you and observe, if you can get me in."

"What? I don't want to go to class, even though I have to be there. And you want to go just for the hell of it? I hate to disappoint you, girl, but it's not much different from high school. Before starting college, I had visions of Socrates on the steps of the Parthenon exchanging deep thoughts with a bunch of brilliant, handsome, tight-assed, homosexual, Greek guys."

"What does homosexual mean?"

"I'll let Daniel explain that one to you. Anyway, the professors are pretty sharp. And while some of the students are smart, most have average intelligence, and some are out-and-out stone stupid. The college board scores of the seniors in my advanced math and French IV classes back at Kiski averaged in the thirteen hundreds, whereas the intelligence level in the general education core in college is much lower. The students are passive, listless and uninterested. It seems like they are wasting their time in college, and a lot of their parents' dough and a lot of the taxpayers' money, too. In the philosophy class, we read Plato's <u>Republic</u>, where he concludes that justice prevails when every person aspires to do what he is most suited to do. I think Plato was right. If most students in college are destined to clean toilets or drill holes into sheet metal, then why is society wasting five years of prime labor and paying for expensive tuition, fees, books and dorms? Imagine what the state budget could achieve if the lower three-quarters of the state colleges were closed and replaced with six-month trade schools."

Chapter XIX

Our cultural geography professor was a cool guy. As I had anticipated, he had no problem with Mary Jane sitting with us, especially since half of the desks were vacant because so many students blew-off class. The professor mistakenly surmised that Mary Jane was my "kid sister", which annoyed Mary Jane.

The professor expended a lot of energy in trying to muster enthusiasm among the students. He changed his inflection and exaggerated his gestures. His performance approached theatrical. Actually, his presentation was insightful and informative. Yet, he still could not get a participatory rise out of the class. I felt sorry for the professor. I pulled out a sheet of tablet paper and wrote, "Professor Klein, … Take it easy. You are doing a great job. You are a very good professor. It is not your fault that the students enrolled are the cast from <u>Night of the Living Dead</u>… An Appreciative Student."

The professor said, "You may be amazed by what I am about to say. Some may be alarmed. Would you believe that our small town is a target for Soviet missiles? Why would the Russians target Indiana, PA, of all places?" The professor paused a few seconds, which seemed like hours, hoping that someone would volunteer a response. His eyes scanned the room, imploring the students to take a stab at his question. Mary Jane stretched and twisted her torso as she also scanned the room. I could tell by the fire in her eyes that she wanted to reply. If not for her undefined status in the classroom, Mary Jane would have immediately volunteered. The professor ended the tension by cold-calling a girl named Tiffany to respond. Tiffany's eyes darted from side to side as she thought, {*With thirty students here, why the hell did he pick me?}* Tiffany asked, "Could… could you repeat the question?"

The professor was deflated by the realization that Tiffany, and probably others, were not even listening to him. He monotoned, "Why would the Soviets target Indiana, PA, with nuclear warheads?"

Tiffany shrugged and started to shake her head as she searched her mind for a good selection of words with which to punt. Before speaking, however, a glimmer came to her face. She brightened as she contemplated a possible response to the professor's question. Angelin and I traded glances. Tiffany was also in our philosophy class. We had heard her speak before. Angelin and I knew that whatever Tiffany would say, it would be a lulu. We were not disappointed. Tiffany broke into a full smile as she proclaimed, "The Soviets are targeting us because Indiana, PA, is the Christmas tree capital of the world."

Angelin wore her best poker face. My eyes watered as I mutilated my tongue within my closed mouth. The professor's jaw dropped. He said, "That's an interesting theory, Tiffany. We don't know for certain the Soviet's nuclear strategy. Who knows the extent of the psychological damage to America if our Christmas tree capital were destroyed. However, experts in national defense all agree that another objective warrants targeting Indiana, PA. Would anyone else wish to contribute to the discussion?"

Mary Jane again twisted to see if a student would bite on the offer. Seeing no hands, Mary Jane boldly raised hers. The professor did not hesitate to engage the irregular.

Mary Jane said, "While riding here today, I saw three large, coal-fired power plants. This small town does not need that much generating capacity. A straight line of towers draped with heavy, electric transmission cables stretches eastwardly to the horizon. Presumably, those lines stretch to New York City, Philadelphia and Baltimore. Could that have anything to do with Indiana's strategic importance?

"Yes, absolutely!" the professor cried with outstretched hands and such exuberance that would have suggested Mary Jane had just scored a touchdown.

⌘⌘⌘

Mary Jane had picked a special day to experience college life. Our philosophy class was moved to a terraced lecture hall where a Presbyterian minister and a Muslim imam compared and contrasted Christianity and Islam. Near the end of the program, the audience was invited to ask questions of the speakers. Mary Jane joined a group of four members from the audience who walked down the aisle and waited in line at a microphone to ask questions. The male questioners courteously deferred to the spunky, young girl who asked the imam to clarify, "Did I hear you correctly when you said that Muslims honor Jesus as a prophet?"

"Yes, you heard correctly," the spiritual leader affirmed.

"I appreciate your efforts toward ecumenical dialogue. But Jesus of Nazareth claimed to be the son of God. If he was right, then he was much more than a mere prophet. If he was the son of God, then he was divine, or God-like. But if he was wrong, then Jesus was the world's most outrageously blasphemous heretic. I really do not see how there can be any honorary middle ground as a prophet. Divinity or blasphemous heretic, take your pick. I was wondering if you could comment on that. Thank you."

The only sound I could hear was the buzz of a fly alighting from head to head two rows in front of me. Mary Jane may have been ready for college. But I doubted whether college would ever be ready for Mary Jane.

⌘⌘⌘

After dropping off Mary Jane when we got home, Angelin followed me to my porch where she waited while I went to my bedroom to fetch her some typing paper. I returned to the porch and gave Angelin the paper. Placing her left palm gently, lovingly, on my chest, she gave me a slow kiss on the cheek and nuzzled my temple. I watched as Angelin skipped down the steps, got into the car and drove off. As I turned to go into the house, I caught a glimpse of Mary Jane sitting on the stone wall aligning the driveway.

"What are you doing down there?" I asked.

"Daniel, I want to talk."

I was instantly gripped by dire anticipation. When Mary Jane took a serious tone, the issues were always quite serious. I could not help thinking that she was going to leave me, again. "Come on up, I will buy you a homemade root beer," I said, faking nonchalance.

The bottom of the bottle was murky with yeast. When you drink a bottle of homemade root beer, you really do not need to eat a meal. Mary Jane made many facial contortions before the words were finally delivered. "I have seen the way Angelin touches you. Are the two of you having sex?" My non-reply was confirmation enough for Mary Jane.

It had only taken a second return trip from IUP for Angelin and me to discover the best use of a car. We had stopped at the reservoir to eat the pizza we had taken out. The car was a portable environment that provided a sense of privacy… Mary Jane followed up with, "Why have you not … you know … made a play for me? Am I that unappealing?"

"Are you kidding? I think you have a hot, little bod. You must sense my interest when we are making out? But you are a bit young for sex, don't you think?"

Mary Jane slammed the pop bottle onto the kitchen table. Mary Jane felt frustrated because her aspirations were repeatedly thwarted by others' perceptions of her that were tainted by her diminutive size. "Tell me," Mary Jane asked, "do you recall Tiffany who gave the 'Christmas tree capital of the world' answer today?"

"I do not think that I shall ever forget Tiffany."

"How old do you think Tiffany is?" Mary Jane asked.

"Nineteen, mayhap twenty."

"Do you think she is having sex?"

"I have no doubt she is," I replied.

"So, you are telling me that Ms. Christmas-tree-capital-of-the-world is mature enough to choose sex, but I lack the intellectual maturity to make that judgment?"

Honestly, she had a point. I said, "Suppose we spend some time touching and exploring. We do not have to go all the way all of a sudden. I have learned that there are a lot of things we can do together that feel really good without risking pregnancy."

ഇന്ദ്രഇന്ദ്രഇന്ദ്ര

"Daniel, you've been delaying this conversation long enough," Mum said as she followed me from the bathroom to my bedroom where I put on a shirt and started to comb my hair.

"Can we talk about this some other time?" I implored. Everyone in Angelin's family had gone to New Kensington shopping. They would be gone for about another hour. Angelin had invited me over to the house for sex. I needed to get over there.

"No, you're already past the earliest date for mailing in applications to colleges. You're jeopardizing the chance at early acceptance to the best schools. You need to jump on this opportunity right now."

"And what best schools did you have in mind?" I knew Mum had something stewing in her mind.

"I think you should go to Williams College."

"Williams? Is that the small, private college where Carolyn's fiancé went?"

"Yes, it is a good school. Rich people send their sons there."

"Oh no, here we go again. Did we not resolve this years ago? Mum, I am not going to bankrupt you by going to a private college. If it was a choice only between a state teacher's college and an ivy league school, I would seriously consider accepting your generous offer. But when you compare the private colleges against a state's flagship research university, I do not think the tenfold cost differential is justified."

"What research university?"

"How about Pitt? What is wrong with Pitt? Jonas Salk developed the polio vaccine at the Pitt labs. The University is flooded with Jewish kids, so how bad could it be? Where is Williams, anyway? New England somewhere? I think it is in Massachusetts. I do not know a soul from Massachusetts. It is a long way from home."

"You mean it's a long way from those girls."

"Oh geez, Mum, please do not start that again. Give me a break."

"Daniel, you are a good-looking boy, smart, from a good family." I chuckled at Mum's self-proclaimed accolade. "I do not know why you waste your time with those girls. They look like they … were bought in the bargain basement."

"Please, Mum, I am begging you …"

"It's embarrassing. Sometimes I think that you date those girls just to upset me."

"What insight you have! You figured it out. All these years with Mary Jane, Joanie and Angelin were for the sole purpose of pissing you off."

"Why don't you give a nice girl, like Jania Jankowski, a call? Her mother wails, 'What's wrong with these boys? Night after night, weekend after weekend, my poor Jania sits at home. She's a good girl. What's wrong with these boys?'"

"Actually, Jania is a very nice girl. And honestly, if I did not have such a full plate … and commitment, I would give Jania a buzz."

"You know, quantity does not outweigh quality."

"I totally agree with you, Mum. That is why I feel thrice blessed," I said while making the sign of the cross.

"Blessed? You're a strange one to use such a word. What an embarrassment. Me, a member of Christian Mothers. Your absence from the church is a scandal. Oh God, tell me why I have failed?"

"I guess you just did not try hard enough. Hey look, I have an urgent … pressing engagement at Angelin's."

"What pressing engagement?"

"She needs to drive to IUP in a couple of hours to take an exam, and she is having some car problems that she urgently needs me to probe."

"What car problems?"

"She is concerned about some strange sounds emanating from her car. But all she probably needs is a lube job. I must go. We will talk later."

Chapter XX

An hour later, Angelin and I sat on a swing under her father's Concord grape arbor, drinking mint tea. "God, I needed that," Angelin said as her eyes swooned. "Sex is a great release of tension. But it's too temporary."

"What is the problem?"

"I don't know. I think I am having a midlife crisis."

"But you are only eighteen."

"Yea, but I am having some sort of transitional anxiety. One day last week, I got up half dazed at the crack of dawn and started to get ready to go to school—I mean to catch the bus to go to Kiski. When I realized that a graduate doesn't catch the bus anymore, I looked out the window and saw the three of you boarding the bus at the corner. It felt weird to not catch the bus. I don't know why, but I started to cry." Angelin picked a grape and placed it in her mouth. Her teeth squeezed out the pulp. She crunched the seed and spat out the tough skin. "Do you remember on Tuesday night when my folks interrupted some very serious touching on the porch? What did you do when you got home?"

"I immediately satisfied my yearnings by handling the matter myself," I said.

"For the very first time, so did I."

"How was it?"

"Pretty good. But the point I'm trying to make is that part of me wants to remain at Kiski. At the same time, my calculus professor at IUP addresses me as 'Miss Bugliese', while my parents restrict me like a little kid. I guess what I'm saying is that I am tired of living at home."

"Where will you go?"

"That's it. I'm not going anywhere. I don't have the money for an apartment. And my folks sure as hell are not going to pay for one. I feel trapped."

ૐૐૐ

Donnie Alberts and Valerie McKenzie were going steady during September and most of October of our senior year. Donnie imitated the devotion of a bird dog during the relationship, while Valerie appeared increasingly disinterested. A few minutes before lunch on a day in late October, Donnie and Valerie were in the clock tower quad at the high school. Valerie stomped as she walked, while Donnie followed and pleaded tearfully, "But I still don't understand why you want to break up." Valerie quickened her pace. Donnie followed. He choked on his words as he said, "Everything was going swell, then bam. Will you talk to me? Why won't you talk to me?"

Valerie stopped so abruptly that Donnie nearly plowed into her. She folded her arms and barked, "Talk."

"Val, you are the most important thing in my life," Donnie sobbed. He looked grief stricken, as if someone had died. "You said you wanted a career where you could help people. Well, I'm people, too. I need your help. I love you and want to be with you forever."

Valerie exuded annoyance bordering on disgust. As she rolled her eyes, she observed that most of Kiski High was looking at her. Valerie reeled towards Donnie and exploded, "Stop it! I'm warning you. Leave me alone." Valerie charged off towards the senior building. She stopped just long enough to shout, "And don't call me anymore!"

Watching the transaction, I knew that I could not stand the risks to which Donnie had subjected himself. I could never be a pursuer. I would either have to be a girl and be the one being pursued, or I would have to be the way I was with les triplés. Since I was not a female, then my only alternative was a lifelong commitment, but it had to be a multiple commitment to a consortium of smart ugly girls.

Chapter XVII

Joanie and Mary Jane hurriedly ate the cafeteria lunch special, which probably was a wise way to make it go away. They were rushing to get to choir rehearsal. Between gulps Joanie said, "Mary Jane and I, along with Angelin, have to go to a wedding shower for Angelin's cousin, Carmen, on Saturday night."

"This seems to have come all of a sudden," I said. "I did not even know Carmen was engaged."

"It has to be all of a sudden," Joanie smirked. "I think it's a combo wedding/baby shower."

I mused incredulously, "Can you imagine being adjoined in holy matrimony for all eternity with Brune Carmen?"

"I think it's just as bad from Carmen's point of view. She's stuck with Terry, the dork of dorks."

Mary Jane broke into a full-bodied satire of Handel's *Messiah*, "DORK OF DORKS, forever and ever, ALLELUIA, ALLELUIA."

I said, "I think I would have an abortion before committing to dork and son of dork."

"Shush," Joanie admonished me. "Don't even utter that foul word." Joanie was a devout Catholic. However, I think her revulsion towards abortion would be just as poignant if she were not Catholic."

Mary Jane giggled and suggested, "OK, then she should carry the baby to delivery and then kill herself."

"You can't commit suicide, either," Joanie protested again in frustration.

"I cannot understand how anyone can become accidentally pregnant," Mary Jane said. "Even Carmen and the Holy Dork understand the mechanics of baby making. Why take the risk? Just do not do it."

"Maybe Carmen wants a baby," Joanie proffered.

"OK, then have a baby," Mary Jane reasoned. "But the mother does not necessarily have to get married."

"That's not the way life is supposed to happen," Joanie moaned. I, however, was intrigued by Mary Jane's insight into an option I had never contemplated.

"Wait a minute," I said. "Why were you two invited? You are not friends of Carmen. You hardly know her, other than by reputation."

"I think she wants the gifts," Mary Jane replied. "She probably needs the gifts. Terry and she do not have a pot to piss in. Besides, I think Angelin is having a hard time collecting a decent party."

"Angelin is throwing the shower?" I laughed. "So, that is why you are going? You have been drafted?"

"You got it, Poncho."

"And how did Angelin get roped into such a central role?"

"Drafted," the chorus sang as they ran off to rehearsal.

As I conducted a postmortem on my lunch platter, Ken Ziska sat down two seats away from me at the same row of tables. Ken said to Cal Jukes, who sat across from him, "Asking a girl out is no sweat. I make a list of twenty girls and their phone numbers, ranging from drop-dead gorgeous to a total skag. I call number one on the list. Of course, I am so nervous I can hardly speak. The thought of rejection nearly paralyzes me. I awkwardly fumble through a brief conversation. The girl turns me down. We exchange goodbyes, and I hang up. But, very importantly, I don't take my hand away from the receiver. While drifting in numbness, I immediately pick up the phone again, and acting like a robot, I dial up girl number two. During the conversation, I feel but a fraction of the nervousness I had with number one. By number three, the nervousness is gone. I actually sound cool in the conversation. I am enjoying the experience. The conversation lasts longer than the prior ones. I don't take the rejection personally. I don't even care whether I am rejected. After all, the rejection is only a part in the script of my sociological / anthropological research on women and dating. Somewhere around numbers four or five, I become extraordinarily witty because I can anticipate much of the conversation. Also, around this time, I score a winner. When I go to bed that night, I feel good about the process. I have a date with a babe, and the rest of it was not a searing personal rejection. It was just research. The worst thing a guy can do is waiting five years to ask a girl out and then, if rejected, not immediately pursue another. If he broods over the one and only rejection in his life, he'll develop into a crazed psychopath."

After delivering my tray onto the return conveyor belt, I made a first-time decision to treat myself to an ice cream dixie cup. While waiting in the ice cream line, I reviewed my jobs schedule listed on the brown pages of a cheap tablet made of visible wood pulp fibers. Since les triplés would be occupied at the wedding / baby shower, I was looking at shifting jobs into Saturday evening and out of Sunday. If successful, all of Sunday could be freed up so I could pal around with les triplés. I thought, "We could watch a movie at the drive-in. Beforehand, we will go to Leo Moore's diner for fishtail sandwiches." Leo Moore was two hundred years old and made the best, and cheapest, fish sandwiches. The thin and wide fillets were batter dipped and deep-fried in bacon lard collected from breakfast preparation earlier in the day.

All of my jobs on Sunday were inside jobs. No customer wanted the neighbors to see me working on the customer's property on the Lord's Day. Some customers, like old Mrs. Olsawski, were willing to let me work inside on Sunday … for a ten-percent discount. I was scheduled for high noon on Sunday to install a handrail aside the steps leading to the furnace and coal bin at Mrs. Olsawski's house. She also wanted me to replace the ceiling light fixture in her kitchen. I contemplated asking Mrs. O to reschedule the work for Saturday evening … with my customary ten-percent discount, of course.

As I surfaced from deep concentration of my schedule, I realized that the ice cream line had not moved. I abandoned the pursuit. Swiftly reeling around to quit the line, I collided with Valerie McKenzie, who, unbeknownst to me, had joined the queue. There she was, the living icon, the image that had launched thousands of masturbation episodes among her classmates of the male denomination. Embarrassed by my absentmindedness, I apologized.

"I was amazed to see you in line, Daniel. I'm here every day and never see you get ice cream."

"This was my first attempt and probably my last. Apparently, no one can find the key to the cashbox. For this to happen today, of all days, is a sign that the gods never intended for me to have ice cream." The quizzical expression on Valerie's face gave me the impression that her English lit class never poetically used the term, god, in a generic sense.

"What were you looking at in that tablet? You were in another world."

"Oh," I chuckled. "I keep the schedule in there of the odd jobs I work. I was trying to rework it to schedule some jobs for Saturday night."

"You are going to work Saturday night? That's ridiculous."

"I really do not have a better alternative for Saturday night," I said.

"Why don't you go to Marna Sweitzer's party?"

"I do not have an invitation to the party."

"Oh, for Pete's sake, I guarantee that you will have one in about five minutes. So, whad'ya say?"

"I … I … don't know," I said with a contraction to avoid sounding like a nerd.

"We're seniors. We're supposed to be partying our brains out. Can you get a car for Saturday night?"

"Uhm … yea, I suppose."

"Good then, you can pick us up at Marcia Cuddy's house at seven-thirty."

"Whoa, you want me to pick you up and take you to a party?"

"I'm not talking about a date. You won't just be taking me. You'll be picking up some friends—me, Marcia and maybe Frank Ashencroft, and then go to a party where there's a lot of people. What's the problem? Won't Joanie Slabovnik let you out to go to a party?"

Chapter XXI

As I drove to Marcia Cuddy's house, I debated with myself, "There is nothing wrong with going stag to a party full of classmates during my senior year… Oh yea? If it is totally legit, then, numéro un—why did you not tell les triplés about it, and deuxièmement—why am a shaking with a hormonal rush?"

Upon arriving at Marcia's house, I discovered that only Valerie, Marcia and Marcia's little brother were home. Marcia had to baby-sit her brother until her parents returned from bowling. She insisted that Valerie and I go to the party without her. Her dad would give her a ride to the party later. When Valerie and I got into the car, I asked, "Why did you have me pick you up at Marcia's? Would it not have been easier to have picked you up at your house?"

"No, that would not have worked out."

"Why not?" I asked.

Valerie cocked her head to the right while using the back of her hand to fling her long golden hair over the shoulder. "Because you are Catholic and, even worse, a Pollack. My parents won't let me date any guy who does not belong to the DeMolay."

"What is the DeMolay?"

"It's a boys' group version of the Masons. You've heard of the Masons, haven't'cha?

"Yea, is that not some brick and stone layers union?"

"No, silly. It's a group of … regular Americans. The men are Masons. The boys are DeMolay. My mother is in the Eastern Star, and I'm an Arrowette. Have you heard of the Arrowettes?"

"I thought it was a colored singing group… And so, these are groups of regular Americans, and that excludes me?"

"Well, yea. You can't be Catholic. A boy in the DeMolay is protestant and something like German or English, Scottish or Dutch."

"Sounds like the Hitler Youth."

"My dad tells me I'm supposed to date guys from the township and not Vandergrift."

I never thought of it, but most of the Anglo-Germans at Kiski were from out of town. Vandergrift was half Italian and half Polish. The men in Vandergrift worked in the steel mill and the foundry.

Valerie directed me to turn onto Reservoir Road. I said, "I do not know where Marna lives. But I did not envision her living out here. Marna lives on Reservoir Road?"

"Yea, sort of. She lives off of a road that is off of a road that intersects this road."

"That does not sound like the most direct route."

"Maybe it isn't. I thought that while we are out here, we could talk," Valerie said.

"Talk?"

'Yea."

"Out here by the lake?"

"Yea."

"Talk?"

"Yea. We've been in the same class for three years. Yet, standing in the ice cream line a few days ago was the only conversation we've had. 'Hi' and the cutest smile while passing in the hallways is all that I've gotten from you for three years."

I turned onto an unofficial pathway that led to a view of the moonlit lake. It was a good spot. It was where Angelin and I lost our virginities.

"A half hour earlier on the day when you were in line for ice cream, did you happen to see the embarrassing scene that Donnie Alberts made—out on the quad?"

"If you are asking whether I was a member of the senior class who went to school that day, the answer is yes."

"Oh God," Valerie sighed as she scrunched her face and wrapped her arms over her head. "That crazy Donnie. Tell me, what did you think of that?"

I did not like being put on the spot, but I responded, "I suppose that I thought that … you and he were not a good match."

"Exactly!" Valerie burst with enthusiasm as she pivoted sidewise to face me. She achieved the position by folding her left leg under her, creating a gap in her skirt that revealed the slightly veiled treasure of all treasures. While outwardly appearing nonchalant, my body was being overrun by raging hormones. Valerie continued, "I'm so glad you understand that. If only Donnie could see the light… Hey, enough of the depressing talk. Let's talk about something important like whether Chelsea will cheat on Eric and sleep with Lance. What do you think?"

"I do not know them. Are they in our class?"

"No, silly," Valerie chided. "They're on *Malibu Surfer*. You know, the fabulous TV show. I never miss it. Oh, I'm sorry. You probably don't have a TV."

"Oh, we have a TV. But no one in my family watches it much. Mum watches the soaps. I watch the news if I am home. Occasionally, I watch *Premiere Theatre*. What is your favorite play?"

Valerie shrugged and replied, "I dunno. What's your favorite?"

"That is a hard judgment to make. The new play by Edward Albee, *Who's Afraid of Virginia Woolf*, might be my favorite. It is so powerful. But overall, I like all the plays written by Tennessee Williams."

"Yuck, you like that hillbilly music?"

"Oh no, you are thinking about Tennessee Jerry Forbes. I am talking about the great playwright, Tennessee Williams, the guy who wrote *A Streetcar Named Desire*, *Cat on a Hot Tin Roof* and *Night of the Iguana*. All are good."

Valerie looked at the rising moon reflected in the lake. "What sign were you born under?"

I was not sure what she meant, but I gave my best shot at a reply, "The sign of the cross?"

"I mean your astrological sign."

"I do not know anything about astrology."

"I could not function without my daily horoscope. You know what it says for today?"

"Enlighten me."

"I am a Gemini," Valerie said. "And today a Gemini should take a risk and be more adventurous."

"But I thought you were a Christian."

"I'm an Episcopalian."

"Isn't there a fundamental inconsistency between astrology and Christianity as to what or who rules fate?"

Valerie shrugged. She pushed up the sweater sleeve of her left arm. While shaking her wrist, she asked, "Do you like my bangle? I bought it this afternoon."

"Wow, c'est très chic. Is it gold?"

"It sure is."

"How much did it cost?"

"I dunno. I just charged it to my dad's account at Zellner's."

"Your folks let you do that?"

Valerie chuckled while replying, "My dad will be a little bent out of shape when the bill comes in. But the way I see it, I deserve it because I'm worth it."

"What are you worth?"

Valerie thrust forward her bangled wrist and ringed fingers while she replied, "I am worth very, very nice things."

"Why?"

"Why what?"

"Why are you 'worth it'?"

"Do you always talk like that?"

"Talk like what?" I asked.

"Weird? … Don't you think I'm worth it?"

Again, I glanced down at the treasure of all treasures and agreed, "Oh yea, you are definitely worth it."

Valerie beamed with satisfaction. She looked again at the lake and said, "I'm taking a risk here, y'know."

"What risk?"

"You are known as the cute guy who dates ugly girls. I wouldn't want people to think I'm an ugly girl." I flinched at Valerie's description of les triplés as ugly, even though it may have been true from an outsider's objective opinion. But still, she did not need to be so cruel by saying it to someone who cared so much about them. "You are always seen with the same three girls, sometimes one alone, sometimes all three at the same time, but no one else. Are you going steady with them?"

"Oh no," I replied. "How do you go steady with three girls at the same time?" Valerie smiled, and I felt crummy. I thought of Peter denying three times his relationship with Jesus.

"So, what do you do with the ugly girls on a moonlit night?"

"I wish you would not call them ugly."

"Saaaar—reee. But doesn't it bother you that you have a bad reputation?"

"No, it does not bother me at all. Actually, there is nothing more personally liberating than having a poor reputation. I can always be me, and I am comfortable with that. Besides, I like being with les triplés."

"Who?"

"The girls… Hey, maybe I should take you to Marna's party now."

"But it's too early. This is an excellent opportunity to do some serious making-out. I am talking serious."

"I am probably going to hate myself in the morning, but I must decline the offer. Look, I will drop you off at Marna's. Then, I am going home."

"Going home? And miss the party? You gotta be kidding. People are expecting you."

"Just tell them something came up."

"Like what?"

"Tell them anything. Tell them I have leukemia. I do not care."

"I just don't understand you, Daniel. You don't want to make out with me. Yet, you want to be with those skaggy girls. I don't see what those girls have that would interest a guy."

"For one thing, they are smart and interesting."

Valerie fumed, "What do those skags know that I don't?"

Valerie's use of the label, skag, royally pissed me off. I twisted sideways to direct the reply, "Each knows the quadratic formula. Do you?"

Valerie raised the right corner of her upper lip and stuck her right index finger in the air and made a twirling motion, implying but not saying, "Big whoopy do."

"OK, let us go in another direction. Each girl can tell me the third person—present tense of the verb 'to be'. How about you? You can give me the answer in English or en Français, your choice. Valerie glared at me. I continued, "You are always listening to music. That is good. You should be able to tell me the notes in a C-minor chord. I will give you a hint. One of the notes is C."

"That's it. I've heard enough. You are too queer. Take me to Marna's."

"By the way, I want you to tell everyone that your dad dropped you off. I do not want anyone to know that I gave you a ride, and absolutely no one is to know about this stop at the lake."

Gawking in disbelief, Valerie said, "Guys usually break their necks to tell the world that they've been with me, even if it didn't happen. You're the first guy to try to keep it a secret, even though we didn't do anything we need to hide. But I can't swear to keep it a secret because this story has way too much scoop value."

"I am warning you, Valerie."

"Like, I'm scared. What would you do?"

"If I hear the slightest whisper about tonight, I will drape a set of rosary beads around my neck and go to your house and talk to your folks. I will tell them that I have changed my mind and that I agree to marry you, but only under the condition that the baby will be baptized Catholic. I will do it. I swear to Jesus I will."

Chapter XXII

As I went to Joanie's house on Sunday to get a haircut, I reflected on the non-date with Valerie the night before. Bottom line: It would be great to have a gorgeous girlfriend—however, I did not think I could be happy with anyone who was not intellectually stimulating. Joanie had seen me coming down the street. She met me on her porch. We hugged and kissed. Joanie asked, "Is your little sister going to adopt Dickens?" Dickens was Joanie's eight-year-old tiger-striped cat whom Joanie had offered to my sister when Joanie had heard that she wanted a kitty.

"No, but thank you very much for the kind offer," I replied. "Marlene took one of the strays from the litter under Mrs. Olsavsky's porch.

"Oh," Joanie said disappointedly.

"I do not understand your wish to give away Dickens. You love Dickens. I see you holding him and stroking him all the time. You have already given away two older cats whom you liked very much, also. I know that you are not trying to end your ownership of kitties because you turn right around and soon pick up a newborn. Why do you give away cats whom you love, just to pick new ones out of a litter?"

Joanie shrugged and pointed for me to sit. I sat on the swing on Joanie's porch while she tried a new haircutting technique she had seen on TV. The great thing about experimentation in haircutting is that the hair always grows back. When she finished, Joanie left momentarily to fetch a razor with which to shave the fuzz on the back of my neck. Upon returning Joanie slapped a folded document onto the vacant portion of the swing beside me. The front of the document was the instruction page for an application to the University of Notre Dame. I turned the front page to reveal an application form already filled out in Joanie's handwriting.

Joanie said, "My dad has finally come to the realization that I'm not going to be a nun. This is Dad's plan B. He's really putting a lot of pressure on me to commit."

"Do your folks have the money for Notre Dame?"

"Barely."

"That is crazy," I said. "Do you know where South Bend, Indiana, is located?"

"It's in Indiana."

"South Bend is close to Chicago."

"How long would it take to get there?"

"That depends on how many flat tires you can reasonably expect to have to change between here and there. It is a full day's drive, which means no weekend visits home. Once you arrive at Notre Dame, you would have to stay there all semester. Do you know anyone else who is going there?"

Joanie threw her hands in frustration. "I thought maybe you would be interested in Notre Dame. After all, you are … well, you were baptized Catholic."

I burst out laughing. I sympathetically shook my head in the negative. "Notre Dame is a good school. Honestly, if it were three miles up the road, I would seriously consider applying to it, especially if I could get a scholarship. But when someone travels across the country to go to Notre Dame, she does it because of the Catholic thing, or he is a rabid football fanatic. Neither of the reasons is sufficient for me. None of our parents is rich. How do we justify bleeding them of their life savings?"

"Oh Daniel, what am I going to do?"

"Negotiate a compromise with your dad. If he is insistent on a Catholic school, then suggest Duquesne in Pittsburgh."

Joanie's eyes doubled in size. "Duquesne doesn't have the star power of Notre Dame. I don't think my dad will be swayed by that suggestion."

"First point, your dad has to compromise some, too. Do not forget that the choice is ultimately yours. But you have to concentrate on the presentation of the idea. Get a copy of the Duquesne application from the guidance counselor at school. When you talk to your dad, make sure your mom is there also. After emphasizing private—Catholic, walk over to your mom, put your arm around her, make your eyes teary and say, 'Staying close to you is the most important reason to go to Duquesne.' Then tell your dad to take a couple of days to think about it. That will give your mom time to soften him up."

Joanie laughed at my choreographing of the strategy. She asked, "But what are your plans, Daniel? And am I a part of them?"

"Coincidentally, I spent a sleepless night thinking about us. We need to talk." I went to the phone inside the kitchen and picked up the receiver, but someone was talking on the phone. Joanie had two neighbors on her party line. I motioned to Joanie to come and listen.

After listening a few seconds, Joanie placed her hand over the receiver and whispered, "It's Mrs. Bonaddio. She could be on all night chewing the rag."

"If she uses it that much, why doesn't she get a private line?"

"Why don't we?" … Joanie spoke into the receiver, "Hello, Mrs. Bonaddio. Hello! Mrs. Bonaddio! This is Joanie from down the street. I am sorry to interrupt your conversation, but I need to make an important call. It will take just …" Joanie looked at me, and I held up two fingers. "…just two minutes, Mrs. Bonaddio. Oh, thank you so much, I really appreciate it." Joanie hung up. We stared at each other for a minute.

"What do you think?" I asked. Joanie shrugged, then nodded. I picked up the receiver and heard silence. I dialed Angelin's number. Luckily, Angelin answered. I said, "Pow-wow at Joanie's in fifteen minutes."

"No way, Daniel. I'm in the bowels of writing the worst bullshit I've ever written for a paper that's due tomorrow morning."

"The topic of the meeting is—Life in September."

"I'll be there." Click.

I ran to Mary Jane's house and collected her. When Angelin

arrived, we sat around the kitchen table. I said, "The topic is the future. Who wants to start?"

Angelin looked at the clock on the wall and said to me, "You called this convention. Why don't you start?"

"OK, I spent all night thinking about this."

"Oh boy," Angelin quipped. "If Daniel spent all night thinking about something, then hold onto your hats, folks. This is gonna be a doozy."

"I propose that we move in together into an apartment in August. Joanie, Angelin and I would move-in in August. Mary Jane will join us when she graduates."

After an eerie moment of silence, Angelin said, "Well, I wasn't disappointed. That's what you spent all night thinking about? While you were in your coma, did you ever contemplate the issue of who the hell in Vandergrift is going to rent an apartment to a single guy and two unmarried girls?"

"We will get an apartment in Pittsburgh, in the Oakland section. Do you remember last month when I visited my sister at Pitt for a weekend? She took me to a football game and a frat party. Well, you will not believe what I saw. I saw a colored man and a white woman living together in an apartment."

"UH—uh!" Joanie exclaimed. "Is that legal?"

"I do not know," I replied. "But it goes to shows you that just about anything goes in Oakland. Most of the people living there are the artsy types. I love it there. I did not see any rednecks. If there are any, they have bigger fish to fry than us."

"So, let me guess," Angelin said. "You expect me to transfer my IUP credits to Pitt?"

"You are too perceptive," I replied.

"And what about Joanie?"

"I hope she eventually goes to Pitt. But there is a good chance she might go to Duquesne, a short streetcar ride from Pitt, down Forbes Avenue."

"Stop! Stop!" Joanie burst in. "This whole idea is insane. We can't live together. People would mistakenly believe that we're having sex." Angelin had gotten up and was behind Joanie, facing the refrigerator to get a jelly-jar full of iced tea. Joanie's words prompted Angelin to twist around. Her mouth gaped as she stared at me sitting across the table from Joanie. Mary Jane and Angelin stared at each other. From behind Joanie's back, Angelin oscillated her pointing index finger between Joanie and me while simultaneously shaking her head, miming the question, "Are you two not having sex?" Mary Jane's eyes were fixated on me as I subtly, almost imperceptibly, shook my head no. Mary Jane's bug-eyes looked askance. Angelin tilted her head back and stared at the ceiling in amazement.

"Why can't we get two apartments or live in the dorms?" Joanie asked.

"That would be twice the rent of one apartment. If we work hard this summer and save a lot, and maybe if we have small part-time jobs while in college, we three collectively can handle the living costs of one apartment without subsidy from our parents. If we handle the living expenses ourselves, then we can enjoy total freedom."

"Absolutely!" exclaimed Angelin as she lunged towards the table, planting both hands upon it. "Believe me. My experiences since graduation have proven that freedom is everything it's cracked up to be. Besides, I don't think my folks could help out much anyway."

"It sounds like you like the idea," Mary Jane said to Angelin.

"I think it's the best brain storm Daniel has ever come up with."

"But what do we tell our folks?" Joanie pleaded.

"You will be a legal adult then. Just tell them the truth," I suggested.

"Don't be ridiculous," Angelin chided me.

"But I can't lie to them," Joanie lamented.

Turning back to Joanie, Angelin said, "Look, Dumb-dumb, you *can* tell them the truth. Tell them that you are getting an apartment with Angelin ...period."

During the discussions I kept glancing at Mary Jane, who looked dejected. I slid my chair over to hers and put my arm around her. A tear rolled down her cheek. She said, "You are abandoning me."

"I would never abandon you," I said softly.

"Yes you are. Why ... wh... why could you not just keep driving to IUP?"

"And live where for two years? At home?"

Angelin interjected, "No way. This week, I had decided that I was going to quit college after this semester."

"Oh no," Joanie gasped.

"I'm dead serious. I was going to tell you sometime this week. I was planning to move into an apartment. And if that required scooping skyscraper ice cream cones and mounds of chipped-chopped ham full-time forever, so be it. But Daniel's plan gives me the incentive to tough it out 'til August."

I added, "By this summer, Angelin will have accumulated forty credits at IUP. If she is ever to transfer, it must be now."

"Oh, this all sounds great for everyone,… except me," Mary Jane sniffed.

I motioned to Joanie to hand me the Notre Dame application setting on the countertop. I set the application in front of Mary Jane and pointed to it. "This would have been abandonment—going to a college so far away that we could not visit on weekends. Let me ask you, if we could immediately jump two years into the future, would you favor the plan?"

"Living together, going to school and being able to go to the theatre and art galleries, having parties? Yea, I think I could get into that."

"So," I asked, "the problem is with the two year hiatus?"

"Yea."

"I like Pittsburgh for several reasons. Primary, however, is being only an hour away from seeing you. I will come home every weekend. We will work together. We will do homework together, we will hang out. When we feel like it, we can go for special car rides." Mary Jane sniffed and grinned, her first grin of the evening. "I will take you to two proms. I will try to load my course schedule for mostly Monday through Thursday. If I can swing it, I will try to blow off some Fridays and come home Thursday evening… And so will Joanie." I pointed to Joanie and asked, "Right?"

"Oh yea, I would want to come home many weekends."

I looked at Angelin but knew better than to ask. I turned back to Mary Jane and said, "Maybe you will be able to come to Pittsburgh on some weekends. That would be great, would it not?"

"It would be fantastic," Mary Jane agreed. "But I doubt if I could get my mother to agree."

"Next year you will be a year older, more mature and independent. By letting you visit us, your mom would also be freeing the weekend for herself if she has special plans. Besides, I think a lot of this depends on how you package the product."

"What do you mean?" Mary Jane asked.

Joanie helped out, saying, "Maybe it would be better if you did not do the asking. Instead, take Angelin and me with you. Your mom may be persuaded more if two college girls asked for her permission directly." I chuckled how Joanie had picked up the fine art of choreographing parent-spin.

"It might work," I opined.

"It might," Mary Jane smiled.

Chapter XXIII

I walked Mary Jane and Angelin home. They chattered like a couple of magpies. While maintaining the pace, Mary Jane athletically shuffled sideways to address me directly, "I cannot believe that you and Joanie have not slept together. Albeit that I am not complaining that you are not having enough sex with other girls. But what is wrong with Joanie?"

"There is nothing wrong with Joanie," I replied. "I assume that she and I will eventually have sex, when it is the right and natural time."

"Right and natural?!" Angelin cried incredulously. "With me, you gave it the full court press."

"That was because I was a virgin at the time and was keen on losing that status at the earliest opportunity. Besides, you were pretty ripe for the picking. And what is so unusual about this anyway? Just as Joanie is now, you also were a virgin during your whole senior year."

"Yea," Angelin conceded, "and in my next lifetime, I won't make that mistake again. I was hot to trot during most of my high school days and wasted too many opportunities for some quality orgasms. And that was your fault." Angelin slapped me in the chest.

ॐॐॐ

Angelin had just returned from visiting her great grandmother at the nursing home. "I'm so depressed," Angelin said to Mary Jane. "I'm depressed every time I return from that place. That'll never happen to me. I will kill myself first."

"We are lucky that Joanie is not here to hear you talk of suicide." Mary Jane chuckled. "How would you kill yourself, slit your veins?"

153

"Oh no, that's too messy. I don't think that I could be brave enough to cut myself. No, I'd use drugs—an overdose—and just drift off to oblivion."

"Probability is against your being successful," Mary Jane said.

"Why won't I be successful? I'm not kidding. I'll really do it."

Mary Jane replied, "I believe that you fully intend to pull the plug before acceding to a vegetative or bedsore state. I just think that it is probable that you will fail. Look at those miserable inmates of a nursing home. The biggest mistake that disabled persons make when it comes to suicide is that they procrastinate too long in assembling the means needed to complete the task. When those people in the nursing home were young, they also encountered decrepit persons, and just like you, each made a promise to herself to end her life with dignity before falling into such a miserable state. Yet, there they are today, suffering in the nursing home. Ninety percent of the inmates of the nursing home would commit suicide today if they had the means. Ten years earlier, each one intended to commit suicide when her condition got too bad. But at some moment in time, she slipped from a marginally acceptable existence into a state of invalidity without having acquired, while she was independent, a stash of death-inducing drugs that she would have used as her last act of a free and independent person. Now, she has no choice. Others are forcing her against her will to live in this hell on earth. They are even using life prolonging procedures to extend the torture beyond the natural term. So, do you have a stash of drugs?"

"No," Angelin replied.

"You talk the talk, but without a stash ready, you are simply bullshitting. Without a stash available, you are doomed to follow your great grandmother into that same house of torture."

⟑⟑⟑

Mary Jane jogged towards Joanie's house with apprehension. She opened the note again and read;

Angelin & Mary Jane,

We need to talk, sans Daniel. Meet at my house 4 PM, Tuesday. If this is inconvenient, call me ASAP.

Joanie

Mary Jane folded the note and placed it into her jean jacket pocket. The sun glared. Déjà vu imposed upon her the sensations of that fateful day when she had thrown down the gauntlet and prodded Daniel to declare an exclusive commitment to her. Mary Jane arrived three minutes late. Angelin was already there. Joanie and Angelin were talking but abruptly ceased upon seeing Mary Jane. A sense of alienation enveloped her. Joanie and Angelin had a special relationship, the likes of which Mary Jane did not have with either of them. When it came to les triplés, Mary Jane was the odd girl out, l'étranger. It had been a strategic error for her not to have come fifteen minutes earlier. Joanie offered Mary Jane a devil's food gob. Although Mary Jane's stomach growled with hunger, she refused, fearing that she could not hold it down.

"Maybe we should have gotten together and talked long ago," Joanie started. "I have gone with the flow for years. But Daniel's plan for all of us to live together is, well, queer." Mary Jane listened but did not react. Joanie continued, "I've been getting the third degree from my mom. Don't get me wrong, my folks like Daniel. Remember that giant oak out front? Some guy offered to take it out for a hundred bucks. I thought my mom was going to have a coronary when she heard that. The company even wanted my folks to sign a waiver releasing the company of liability if the tree would hit the house. Daniel spent three days cutting it down for free. He scared me to death when he climbed to the top branches and systematically cut pieces from them."

"I remember that," Angelin said. "He looked like a monkey up there. So, what problem does your mom have with Daniel?"

"Oh, she likes him swell enough. She just thinks that the relationship discourages potential suitors. She is worried that I will not have a date for the prom."

Sophomore Mary Jane did not catch the significance, but graduate Angelin burst into laughter. Angelin said, "It's not even Christmas, yet prom hysteria is already gripping the senior class?"

Joanie said to Angelin, "I told Mom that although Daniel took you last year, he would take me this year because it is our senior year. Even so, my mom's best friend, Sophie Stopanyak, is concerned that her son, Jerry, has never been on a date."

"You are saying that guys' moms get worried if their sons have not had a date?" Angelin asked.

"I guess so. The whole world is crazy. Anyway, Sophie says to son, Jerry, [Joanie used a mocking nasal voice] 'Why don't you ask out Joanie Slabovnyk?' Jerry tells his mom that I am 'already taken by Daniel.' Now my mom is pushing for me to do something."

"Do what?"

"To pressure Daniel to shit or get off the pot when it comes to commitment."

Mary Jane closed her eyes and smiled as she leaned her head back onto the top of the chair back. She thought, {*Déjà vu all over again.*}

"Are you interested in Jerry Stopanyak?" Angelin asked.

"No, I do not know. But I have a dream. Just once, for my self-preservation and for my dignity, I want to be asked out. Look, I would not mind being asked out by the son of Frankenstein just for the experience. Mary Jane and Angelin nodded in empathy. "Isn't it a woman's birthright of American citizenship to have one guy who is committed to you and you alone, one on one?"

"So, what do you want to do?" Mary Jane asked.

"We need some sense of where we are going with our lives. Les Triplés has been fun, and so is the idea of sharing an apartment. But that is yet another scheme that will hold us in this relationship limbo. Maybe Mom is right. Maybe the love of my life is out there, and I am missing him because I carry around a 'property sold' sign called Daniel. I am hidden in les triplés. Les triplés may be OK for Daniel, but ..."

{*Déjà vu all over again.*}, Mary Jane thought.

"So, what do you want us to do?" Mary Jane asked.

"Let's make an agreement to draw lots to see who gets Daniel. The losers graciously walk away. What do you think?"

Angelin replied, "Did I tell you that I had an offer for a date?"

"No, that's great, Angelin," Joanie lauded encouragingly.

"Perhaps the term 'date' is not totally accurate. Actually, it was an offer to have sex on a regular basis. His name is Giuseppe, a friend of my father. He's fifty years old, married, balding, five foot—one, two hundred and eighty pounds. The few teeth he has are stained with chewing tobacco, and his breath reeks of garlic. Then on the other hand, his English is notsa hot. He wants an arrangement to meet at lunchtime once a week. Dante's image of hell was mild compared to my nightmare of being chained to a bed for all eternity with Giuseppe breathing on me. I look at Giuseppe, and I look at Daniel, and it's hard for me to believe that they are members of the same specie. Right now, I have an exclusive date with Daniel at least one weekend night a month, plus I get to hangout with les triplés ninety-five percent of the rest of the time. When I am with Daniel, he treats me like a princess. I'm really looking forward to the apartment in August. You expect me to give up all of that for a sixty-seven percent probability that I will be either alone or with Giuseppe? That sounds like a poor choice. Besides, Squirt [referring to Mary Jane] is part of the equation. Implicit in the agreement is that the two losers would absolutely relinquish all claims to Daniel and walk away. How could Squirt be part of the deal? She may express assent, but she would mean it only if she wins. If Mary Jane wins, she will demand our compliance. But if she loses, she will renege. She…"

"Angelin is right," Mary Jane interrupted. "Last year I would have entered the agreement with no intention of complying if I lost. But today, I will not even entertain such a sham. Today, I am not insulted by your fair indictment of my past character. But in the future I will not accept such slander. I shall never give up Daniel. Even if I had an entourage of men swooning after me, I would still choose Daniel. Les triplés is an acceptable arrangement for me… There is another factor you have failed to consider, Joanie. From first hand experience, I do not think that Daniel would accept our decision if it meant ending les triplés. Daniel has never been with just one girl. I think les triplés is not a coincidence. If two girls walked away, then purposefully or unconsciously, Daniel would recruit replacements who have not experienced the benefits we have enjoyed for years and who will not take them for granted."

Joanie's motion died from a lack of a second.

Chapter XXIV

Imprints of Joanie's features protruded through her tank top. They always became prominent when she was cold. Les triplés wore their skimpies and flimsies so as to cope with the scorching heat outside. However, the sarcophagus that was the stone bank was cold. Each of us filled in an application for a bank savings account. I also applied for a checking account, my first. We giggled as we exchanged weird suggestions for answers to the questionnaire. Everyone giggled, save Joanie, who seemed to believe that one should manifest reverence while abiding in a stone edifice. "Hush up," Joanie said in a loud, sharp whisper. "You guys sound like a pack of hyenas." Angelin, Mary Jane and I continued to joke and giggle. "How come you guys aren't taking me seriously?"

Mary Jane giggled through a reply, "It is hard to take someone seriously when she is mounted with two attack torpedoes." Joanie sank her shoulders forward and crossed her arms around her chest.

"That's OK," Angelin added, "you can negotiate a better interest rate for all of us."

Our more important mission for the day was to hunt for an apartment. Over the summer, we had amassed a mighty war chest with which to launch the invasion of Pittsburgh. Saving money was second nature to me. But the zeal of the girls to work and save money to support the move was unexpectedly impressive. Even Mary Jane tendered a token donation, even though she would not be joining us fulltime for another twenty-one months.

A string quartet performed on the lawn of the Cathedral of Learning. Oakland was in a festive mood. And les triplés were happy to be there. Angelin was age nineteen. Joanie and I were eighteen. And

Squirt, as Angelin pejoratively referred to Mary Jane, was only sixteen. It would have been easy for any of us to be fearful of moving away from home. But the collective courage of les triplés was strong. We believed that we could achieve anything as long as we stuck together. Certainly, we could handle the financial burden of one household, or apartmenthold. Les triplés were not leaving home. Les triplés *were* home. Wherever we were, as long as we were together, we were home. So, moving from Vandergrift was not traumatic because les triplés were merely colonizing a small part of Pittsburgh.

Shopping for an apartment was entertaining. To our surprise, the landlords did not bat an eye when we presented a guy and two girls as the lessees. Due to our ages, however, we sometimes had to show our bank books to prove our financial wherewithal. We looked at three-bedroom apartments. A controversy arose over where Mary Jane would sleep when she would visit. Angelin and Joanie kept volleying between them the proposition that Mary Jane should sleep in the other's room. The bickering made Mary Jane feel as if she would be a burden and not a fully enfranchised member of les triplés. Everyone would have her own bedroom, except for Mary Jane. I tried to resolve the matter by proposing that Mary Jane could sleep with me when visiting. That caused all hell to break lose.

In the evening, we looked at an apartment about a half mile from the Pitt campus. The maintenance man who would normally show the apartment was out for the evening. But a new guy from the realty management company was there doing the monthly maintenance check. We showed the realty guy the classified ad in the newspaper. He surmised that the ad must have been referring to apartment 214, the only one of which he knew was vacant. He had a set of keys, so he showed us the apartment. The living room was nice, but the first bed-room was spectacular. It was the largest bedroom I had ever seen, with a bay window along one wall and another large window along a wall perpendicular to the bay window. While the location of the apartment had bustling city streets a block away in every direction, the side street onto which the bay window viewed was quiet and lined with giant sycamore trees. "This will be my room, Darling," Angelin declared as she strolled like a movie star.

"Why you?" Joanie contested.

"Because I'm the oldest, and because I'll disembowel anyone who disagrees with me."

I thought to myself that the dispute was moot because the apartment was too grand for it to be within our price range.

"Let's see the other rooms," Joanie said, hoping that the other bedrooms would be as quaint. We opened the second door to the bedroom and walked into a small windowless room that smelled of cedar. "This smells like a gigantic cedar chest," Joanie exclaimed.

"That's what it is, Miss," The realty man said. "This is a walk-in closet. It's lined with cedar to hold down the moths." The shelf space starting at neck level was abundant. Along all of the walls combined, there were perhaps thirty feet of clothes hanger rail. Les triplés loved the apartment. The only problem was that we could not find any more bedrooms. The building maintenance man arrived while we were there. He told the realty agent and us that the advertised three-bedroom apartment had been rented earlier that morning to a cellist and pianist with the symphony. The rent on the large one-bedroom was $108 a month, a titch high for one bedroom, but at least twenty bucks less than the crummiest three-bedroom apartments. Angelin suggested that she and Joanie could each have a bed in the bedroom and that I could sleep in the walk-in closet. Although I was extremely modest in expectations for my personal comfort, I felt that the windowless closet would fall below even my Spartan standards. Yet, to be fair, I went back into the closet and sniffed the cedar. I tried to imagine myself in there, night after night, for years. I was not claustrophobic, but the closet made me think of Anne Frank's diary. Besides, I had to assess my role as the guarantor of rent payments. I believed that Joanie would consistently provide her share of the rent. But I was under no delusion that Angelin would consistently provide her share by the due date. Angelin would have the best intention to pay her fair share on time. I just doubted whether she would make it. And I was certain that she would not make the payments consistently. Only I had the reservoir of cash that could, within a moment's notice, fill in the inevitable shortfalls of others. And as the guarantor of rent payments, I figured that I deserved sleeping in a room with a window. We had to choose a different apartment.

After walking a block from the apartment, I noticed that I was walking alone. Les triplés had stopped fifty yards behind. They were in whispered caucus. They broke the gathering and walked swiftly towards me. They passed me without stopping. Mary Jane yelled back to me, "We are going to the drugstore on the corner, and then we must find a restroom. Stay there, we will meet you there later."

As I waited at the intersection of the quiet tree-lined street, I saw a bus collect a passenger a block away—at the intersection where the drugstore was located. Thirty seconds later, a streetcar discharged two old ladies at the same intersection. A minute later, a second streetcar stopped. "Wow," I thought, "how convenient. On most streetcar routes, a passenger must depend on a schedule. If either the streetcar or passenger is late, the passenger incurs a lot of wasted time. But since all of the routes east of the city merge and funnel through Oakland on the way downtown, a trolley or a bus is always available if the passenger wants to go downtown. This part of Oakland resembles a subway system of a large city. You just go to the stop, and a trolley appears, no schedule and no waiting. This would be a convenient location from which Joanie could catch a ride to Duquesne University.

We had planned to save some money by going back to the car and retrieving some snacks, rather than eating out. But as we turned the corner onto Craig Street, we saw a pizza shop that had on the sidewalk three tables under umbrellas. Angelin loved outside cafés, so I was not surprised when she said, "I'm a hungry bear. How expensive could a pizza be, anyway?" That was all the coaxing les triplés needed. Looking over the menu, Angelin asked, "What's the cheapest way to order pizza?"

Since I was the Director of Cheapness within les triplés, I presumed that Angelin was directing her question to me. I replied, "Quantity discounts are usually offered as the pie gets larger. The cost per unit of area is inversely related to the size of the pie. So, do not buy multiple small pies."

Angelin turned to Mary Jane and asked, "Do you have any frick'n idea what he just said?"

"Yea, the cost per square inch decreases as the size of the pie increases."

"Explain it to me in four words or less."

Mary Jane thought a moment and then said, "Buy one big pie."

The largest pie on the menu was called a *wagon wheel*. "What do you want on it?" I asked Joanie.

"I don't care,… cheese."

"Angelin, what do you want?"

"I'm so hungry, I'll eat anything."

"OK then," I said. "Mary Jane, it is your call."

Mary Jane smiled as she extended her arms and splayed her fingers. She ordered, "A pitcher of root beer and one wagon wheel with cheese and double anchovies."

After we each had filled a tumbler of root beer, I announced, "I hate to impose on this gay atmosphere, but we are going to have to choose right now among the five apartments that we saw today."

Joanie said, "I didn't like any of them, except the last one that has only one bedroom. I don't think that we can choose today."

"I agree with Joanie," Angelin said. "However, the apartment market is robust here in August. Vacant apartments do not last long. If we go home right now, today's effort is wasted."

"Oh," Joanie clarified, "I am indeed implying that today's a bust, and we'll have to come again and look at a new batch of apartments."

I commented, "Starting from base zero would be costly, least of which is gas and oil for the round trip. More importantly, we would lose wages. For example, I have a full day of jobs scheduled tomorrow. Do you work tomorrow? How about you? And you? The accumulated wages lost from all of us combined for just one weekday could pay a third of a month's rent. That is pretty costly. And for what? There is no guarantee that we will do better than what we saw today anyway. I say that we weigh the choices we saw today and choose one, right now. I thought the one on Dithridge was …OK."

"Oh no," Joanie cried, "that's the place where the hallway smelled like puke."

"And there were biology projects incubating in the bathroom," Mary Jane added. Everyone shuddered at the thought.

"OK then, how about the place on Neville Street—the one with the green curtains?" I proffered.

"Cockroach!" Joanie declared. "I saw a cockroach in the kitchen."

"How many did you see?" I asked. "I mean, if you only saw one…"

"No, Daniel. I'm not living there—no negotiation."

"Then what about the other apartment on Neville, the corner place?"

"Street noise," Mary Jane noted. And indeed, I had to agree with her.

"That was the place with the landlord with the poppy eyes," Joanie said. "He kept staring at my … my … tits."

"Everyone's been staring at your tits!" we chorused.

"You guys, why didn't you tell me before we left this morning? I could have changed. Thanks a lot, buddies."

"I thought you were trying to make a feminist statement," Mary Jane retorted.

"I thought you intended to permanently engrave the image of yourself in the minds of all the inhabitants of Pittsburgh," said Angelin.

"We are never going to find an apartment acceptable by you guys," I lamented.

"I liked the one bedroom apartment with the bay window," said Angelin.

"And the walk-in closet," said Joanie.

"I am not going to live in a closet," I insisted.

Mary Jane said, "Guys, if we all like it so much, we should get the apartment, and then we all should have a bed in the quaint bed-room… Daniel, is there room enough for four beds?"

I was awe struck, again, by Mary Jane's ability to think beyond our programmed social norms. "Ah, yea, four single beds would fit easily in that huge room, plus one bureau with a mirror is all the furniture we would need in the bedroom because we could easily keep all of our personal stuff in the walk-in closet…Does that apartment come with a basement locker? Did the manager mention a locker? We could keep bikes in a locker. Pittsburgh has steep ridges everywhere. But Oakland and Shadyside are on a plateau that is fairly level and excellent for bike riding."

"I love it. I love it!" Angelin squealed This is gonna be like having a slumber party every night, except … no parents. I love it."

"Control yourself, Angelin," Joanie chided. "Have all of you gone daffy? It was bizarre enough to accept the idea of a guy living in the same apartment, but to share the same bedroom…?" Everyone, save Joanie, rolled their eyes. Angelin almost challenged Joanie's feigned modesty, but retreated because Angelin would have been breaking an implied confidence. A month earlier, Joanie had intimated to Angelin that she and Daniel had come to know each other in the biblical sense many times during the spring and summer. And now, Joanie's display of indignation about seeing Daniel in his boxer shorts seemed highly hypocritical.

Joanie continued, "What would my folks think if they found out? Mary Jane, how can you even contemplate such a notion? What would your mother say?"

"Frankly, my dear, I don't give a damn what my mother thinks. I am not my mother. And I shall not live her life. I benefit from the example of her life experiences for they provide me with a clear chart of what to avoid in my life. I have learned that I need to evaluate life's options and to consider options that others have not. Sometimes, like today, the best option is blatantly obvious, but everyone is blinded to it by their inculcation into ridiculous social norms. We need to exercise our intellect and to trust it. I shall trust my own judgment and make my own rules based on reason, regardless of the number of people who insist upon the opposite. I shall assume a risk, when warranted. We must have the courage to take the step when our reason tells us that the choice is right. So, Joanie, how did I come up with such an outlandish idea like having us all sleep in the same bedroom? It was the most blatantly obvious conclusion. One, we all love the apartment. Two, it is below our budget for a three-bedroom apartment. Three, there is ample room for us all. And most importantly, there is no moral reason not to do it. You cannot imagine how I envy your legal freedom. An arbitrary quirk in the law has incarcerated me within the ludicrous whims of my mother. Over the next twenty-one months, I will lie and do anything necessary to gain a respite here with you, and you, and you. I would give anything to be you right now. And if I were, I would exercise my freedom of majority to the fullest. I would have no dilemma. I would not lie. I would openly live the life of les triplés for everyone to see. Les triplés is good for me and harms no one. And if anyone has a moral issue with that, then she may just go screw herself."

Angelin cleared her throat and said, "Pukey hallway, roaches, poppy-eyed managers staring at your tits… I'm sorry, Joanie, but you get only so many veto cards, and you have just used up your allotment. I second Mary Jane's motion. All of us being together in that fabulous apartment is a great idea. We should do whatever it takes to make it happen. And I think we'll have fun."

I was extraordinarily impressed with Angelin's rhetorical maneuver. I noted to myself that I should try it sometime against an overly negative opponent in an argument: I am sorry, sir, but you have used up your allotment of challenges.

"Well, guys," Joanie said with a hint of exhaustion. "I've got a problem. It's like going to the optometrist who positions two beams of light in two different corners of your vision field and then asks you to merge them. For months, I've been trying to merge two divergent realities, and I don't think that I can do it anymore."

"For the love of the Blessed Mother," Angelin moaned, "is there anyone in this group who doesn't speak in a metaphor? Now, tell me your problem using the most direct language possible, or I'll strangle you."

"I have good news and bad news," Joanie said. "The good news is that after working on my dad all summer, I finally convinced him that it would be cheaper to go to Pitt. I have an appointment next Tuesday with an advisor to try to stitch together a schedule out of the potluck courses that may still have some available seats."

"That is great, girl," I said as I leaned sideways and gave Joanie a hug. "I will make you a copy of my course schedule. Try to get the advisor to use some muscle to get into as many of my courses as possible. And when I see your schedule, if additional seats are available, I will try to drop/add into some of your courses that are consistent with my schedule. Make sure you sign up for French III, section six. Et vous aussi, Angelin, enrôlez en Français troisième."

"Non, Daniel," Angelin replied. "That is a luxury I can ill afford. I have arrived at the point where I must restrict my schedule to a full helping of courses in my major, like organic chemistry."

I asked, "Did you know that the organic chemistry book is the highest prized commodity of the stolen book fencing operations?"

"I'll bet. I know you can rupture yourself by just lugging it around." Angelin then turned to Joanie and made a metaphor of her own, "Now that you've fed us the morsel of good news, it's time for the main course."

"OK. In trying to sell Pitt to my folks, they were strongly influenced by the claim that Angelin would be my roommate. They really liked that because of what happened to my cousin, Caz, last year. Caz was a freshman and signed up for a dorm room, but did not designate a roommate. So, he was assigned a roommate from the pool. Caz's roommate came from a bad part of town and was called by his nickname, Pimp. Pimp threatened that Caz would be "f_ _ _ _ _ up" if Caz entered his own room anytime from Thursday through Sunday, which was the time Pimp had his women there. So, my folks are super glad that Angelin is rooming with me. Now, please understand, I did not lie to them. But, they made an inference, which I never corrected, that since we are *rooming* together, and since I am a freshman, then Angelin and I would be roommates in the dorms. So, that's my dilemma; my folks think that I'll be in the women's dorm, and we're talking about an apartment where I'll be sleeping in the one and only bedroom with Daniel in there. What am I going to do?"

There was a moment of silence as les triplés exchanged glances and contemplated a solution. Mary Jane said, "So, it is a matter of perception. So, why not simply let your parents continue with the uncorroborated inference that you are in the dorms?"

"But my mom will write to me almost every day. She'll expect to be sending her letters to a campus address."

"OK, OK," Angelin said. "That's not a problem. That's not a problem because … Daniel, why isn't that a problem?"

"Ah … Marna … Marna Sweitzer is going to Pitt, and she will live in Holland Hall—South. Marna's a good egg. I bet she will let you have your family address the letters to her suite in Holland Hall."

"Would I have to go up there every day to see if I got any letters? That would be a hassle for Marna and me."

I replied, "Marna and I are in the same calculus class. I will see her twice and—depending upon our GA section—maybe three times a week. I can collect the mail then."

"So, you want me to lie to my family about where I live?"

"No," Mary Jane responded. "The distinction between lying and truth-telling is usually a function of how the statement is drafted." Mary Jane concentrated a moment and then said, "Say to them—quote: The mail is to be sent to this address… end quote."

I burst out laughing and said, "My Lord, we are going to have to send you to law school."

Mary Jane cocked her head and said, "Peut-être." Then she winked at me. At that very moment, I was overcome by a revelation that I had been suppressing for a longtime. But, undeniably, there it was. I would never disclose it to anyone, not even Mary Jane. After all these years, Mary Jane was my favorite, and I was madly in love with her.

"That's slicing the moral baloney pretty finely, isn't it? Joanie quipped.

"It is your moral baloney, not mine," Mary Jane retorted.

Joanie turned to Angelin and asked her, "Do you think I would be lying?"

"No, you are not lying. My definition of lying falls somewhere between Mary Jane's technically strict construction and your moral subjectivity. For me, lying requires that I know a statement to be false, coupled with a harm to the person being deceived. For example, if you said that you did not steal my money when you indeed had, then you would be lying. However, if I said that Joanie's orange madras shirt is très chic, then, under my definition, I would not be lying?"

"What happens when my parents come down to visit?" Joanie asked.

"Meet them in the lobby of the dorm," I answered. "While Holland Hall has restricted access, you do not have to be a resident to sit in the lobby."

"Then, is it agreed, the apartment with the bay window?" Angelin asked.

Mary Jane set her left fist onto the middle of the table and proclaimed, "D'accord."

I laid my fist on top of Mary Jane's and said, "D'accord." Angelin and a reticent Joanie followed suit. We swiftly walked back to the apartment building.

"Do you think the building super will talk to us this late in the evening?" Joanie asked.

"Since he lives in an apartment there, I think he will," I said. "I bet he does this all the time."

"We're probably wasting our time. No one is gonna rent a nice place to anyone as young as we. I bet our application will be rejected."

"I bet you an hour's massage that we have no problem getting the apartment," I wagered.

"You're on," Joanie accepted.

ॐॐॐ

As Angelin and Joanie signed the application, I said to the building superintendent, "We are from out of town, so correspondence between us would take a lot of time. Perhaps we can save a step if I issue a check with the application. If the application is rejected, the check could simply be destroyed." The superintendent agreed that the check was a good idea to speed up the process. I wrote out my first check and handed it to the superintendent. He glanced at the check and did a startled double-take. I explained, "We are serious students and do not want to be distracted by having to worry about making the rent payment during the first several months at university."

"I'll take this application downtown first thing in the morning," the superintendent promised.

Chapter XXV

By unanimous vote, les triplés authorized Joanie to move her cat, Merlin, to the apartment. We chose Saturday to go shopping for beds. Joanie and Mary Jane were off from work, and Angelin swapped work schedules with a co-worker. Angelin would wrap up chipped-chopped ham on Sunday instead. It was another field trip to Pittsburgh—downtown. We would have preferred to have given the business to a Vandergrift merchant, but we wanted to make sure that the store would deliver the beds to our apartment in Pittsburgh. In the interest of financial conservatism, we decided to delay furnishing the living room. However, we had already purchased a bureau with a mirror and a kitchen table and chairs from Tommy McCain's Aunt Jen. Her husband, Pete, had died from a brain aneurism. He never knew what hit him. Aunt Jen was selling her house and most of the furniture and appliances in it.

At the entrance to the furniture store were displays of canopied beds. Joanie lost all control and started bouncing on one, pleading like a little kid, "I've always wanted a canopy bed. Can I get one? Can I get one?"

"Surely you may," I said, "if you are going to live in a tent in the park."

"Ah, poopy-do."

"You have a choice, chicklet, between going to college and buying the bed."

"Oh, Daniel, do not tempt me so."

I suggested bunk beds, but that was vetoed by all three. We saw a bed the size of an aircraft carrier. The salesman called it a king-sized bed. "Do you have sheets to fit such a humongous bed?" Joanie asked.

"Of course," the salesman replied. "We can't sell a bed unless we have sheets for it."

I interrupted, saying, "We are interested in single beds that can be delivered to an apartment in Oakland."

"Right this way."

The salesman showed us a single bed that was firm, comfortable and reasonably priced. One by one, I caught the eye of each girl for affirmation. I said to the salesman, "we wish to buy four singles."

"Great!" the salesman rejoiced with the clap of his hands. "Excuse me a minute while I check the storeroom."

I glanced down at Angelin's watch. I thought, {*If we leave Pittsburgh now, I will have time to change the oil and spark plugs and set the timing points before showering and picking up the girls to go to Marna's party tonight.*}

The salesman returned and pointed to the single bed in front of us and said, "Hey guys, that's the only single bed in this building. We had a ton of them ten days ago. But the college kids have been snapping them up."

Les triplés wearily glanced at each other. "Yea, tell us about it," Angelin huffed.

"We'll get a new shipment in late September."

"That's too late for us," Joanie said.

"How about some double beds?" the salesman suggested.

"Could we get one single and three double beds into the bedroom?" Angelin asked me.

"Yea, but it would be pretty junky looking, a real obstacle course. The three doubles will cost more money. Besides, who would get the single?" Angelin and Joanie immediately glanced at Mary Jane, of course.

"Look," I said, "it would still be a squeeze, but how about one single—and I will take it—and two doubles?"

"Sure," Joanie replied. "But where will Mary Jane sleep when she visits?" Angelin and Joanie pointed to each other.

"OK," I said. "Then I will take one of the double beds, and Mary

Jane will sleep with me when she visits." Having said that, all hell broke loose. I turned to the salesman and said, "We are undecided on this matter. We will look around, and perhaps we will return." While we left the store, I was apprehensive of our prospects with other stores. We were leaving the largest furniture store in Pittsburgh. I expected to find similar shortages of single beds at the other stores. We went to two other stores that had also sold out of their single beds for the month. Angelin was losing steam, so we looked for a cheap restaurant at which we could refuel. We selected Ali Baba's smorgasbord lunch special. We had never eaten at a near eastern restaurant. I found interesting the name, Ali Baba, from the *Arabian Nights,* juxtaposed to the Swedish word, smorgasbord. I guess America really is the melting pot. When the waitress attempted to seat us, Angelin objected and insisted that we be seated at the other end of the restaurant. After we moved to a distant location, Joanie asked, "What was wrong with the other table?"

"There was a toddler seated right next to that table," Angelin replied.

"But look how cute he is, and he's so well behaved."

"Well behaved at this second, Angelin said. "But a toddler can crank up and let loose in an instant without warning. It would be different if the restaurant was paying us a fortune to put up with the ear piercing screaming. On the contrary, I pay money for a pleasurable dining experience. Why should I be subjected to such an annoyance?"

"Do you think your own babies are not going to engage in irritating behavior?" Joanie asked.

"Oh, I expect my babies will be screeching hellions. But they will be my babies, so I'll have to put up with them. That does not mean that I'm willing to have someone else impose her screaming child on me when I am in a public place and paying money for it. I do not think that I owe a public duty to that lady over there to have to endure annoyance from her child just because she wants to go to a restaurant with that uncontrollable child in accompaniment."

Almost immediately the child started babbling in a loud voice. Five minutes later, a shriek arose from the other side of the room, followed by loud wailing and more shrieks. Angelin raised her eyebrows in an implied I-told-you-so. The mother continued dining throughout the meal as if the tempest was not happening.

"Has anyone tried to invent a child muzzle?" I asked.

"Daniel," Joanie said admonishingly, "that would be cruel and inhumane."

"I am not suggesting a device that would hurt the child. I am saying that perhaps there could be a design for a device that could prevent the screaming without hurting the child."

"I am disappointed in you, Daniel, and you too, Angelin."

Angelin and I glanced at each other as co-indicted conspirators of crimes against humanity, according to Joanie's assessment. "OK," I said, "then no muzzle, but how about a muffler worn to deaden the sound? The kid would look like some alien from outer-space. A strapped-on muffler would not hurt the child. In fact, he could enjoy screaming his lungs out. But the sound would be captured in a honey-comb of sound-deadening materials." I grinned broadly with the satisfaction of having manifested ingenuity. But Joanie failed to appreciate it.

We liked the food and ate enough of it. So many of the dishes had a mashed bean base, I figured les triplés would be gastrointestinally ripe by the time of Marna's party.

Mary Jane said, "Joanie, I have not heard you mention in what you will be majoring in college."

"That's because I have not fully decided. But I'm leaning towards teaching, maybe high school English, or maybe French."

Angelin drew her famed poker face. "Excusez-moi," Angelin said while she stood up to go to the restroom. As she walked behind Joanie, Angelin twisted to look back at Mary Jane and me. She mimed two fingers down her throat, conveying her disdain of teaching as a career choice. However, Angelin performed the mime too convincingly. She almost actually caused a regurgitation of garbanzo bean hummus. Mary Jane and I could not control ourselves from bursting into laughter.

"What are you laughing at?" Joanie demanded as she peered behind her and saw Angelin walking towards the restrooms."

"Oh, that Angelin is such a card," I snickered. "She just blew a kiss towards the vocal toddler."

When Angelin returned, Joanie asked, "What are we going to do about beds?"

"I bet we could find them around Vandergrift," Angelin said. "How about that store in Kittaning?"

"I think we can find beds back home," I said. "But how do we get them to the apartment? Do any of you know someone with a truck?"

"Couldn't we carry them on the roof of the car?"

"Yea," I replied, "awkwardly, and maybe one box spring and mattress per trip. That would require four round trips from Vandergrift to Pittsburgh. With a half hour of loading and unloading at each place, we are talking twelve solid hours total for at least two of us. And one of those persons would presumably be I. What a hassle!"

Angelin said, "I think it's time for another of Mary Jane's thinking outside of the box."

"Are you sure you can handle my ideas twice in the same week?" Mary Jane quipped. "For four unmarried persons, conventional wisdom would have hearkened to arguments for an apartment with more than one bedroom. Yet, we have defied conventional wisdom. I am willing to accept any sleeping arrangement because I am so totally satisfied with everything upon which we have already agreed. But, if you really want to know, I think the most aesthetically pleasing arrangement for that magnificent bedroom would be to have one of those mammoth, king-sized beds that we saw at the first furniture store."

"And what else?" asked Joanie.

Angelin laughed as she said, "I think Mary Jane means only one bed. We all sleep on the same humongous bed."

"What?! What?!?" Joanie choked.

"I want an end position," Angelin declared.

"Did you see the size of that bed," Mary Jane said. "We all would comfortably fit on it."

"I get an end spot."

"Are you all mad?" Joanie exclaimed. "Just because Daniel and I are sleeping together doesn't mean that he and I can sleep together."

"Your philosophy of logic professor is going to love you," Angelin noted…"I get an end spot."

"You're easily enough swayed as long as you get the spot you want," Joanie said to Angelin. Turning to me, Joanie pleaded, "Daniel, we haven't heard from you. What do you think?"

Angelin threw her place mat into the air as she roared with laughter. "That is by far the dumbest question I've heard in my whole frick-'n life. For the love of the Blessed Mother, Joanie, he's a guy. He's just died and ascended into Daniel's version of heaven."

Joanie's stare begged a reply from me, which was "I believe that Angelin's comment captures the essence of my opinion on the proposal."

"I'll tell you what, Joanie," Mary Jane said. "The furniture store has one single bed. I would be willing to amend my motion to one king-size bed and one single."

"Well, who would sleep on the single?" Joanie asked.

Mary Jane and Angelin frowned at each other and said in unison, "You would."

"No!!" cried Joanie. "I'm not going to be the only one banished to a single bed."

"I give up," Mary Jane sighed.

"What would my parents think?" Joanie moaned.

Angelin said to Mary Jane and me, "If you guarantee me an end spot in the bed, I think I can convince Joanie to get on board."

"OK by me," I said. "I do not care where I sleep."

"Moi aussi," said Mary Jane, "the choice of sleeping spots is between you and Joanie."

"Okie Dokie." Angelin turned to Joanie and said, "Suppose we pushed on, haphazardly getting a single bed here, another elsewhere and moving them to the apartment. And suppose your folks were to discover that you are living in an apartment off-campus and sleeping in a bedroom with all of us, including Daniel, but in separate beds. What would your folks say? Would they say 'God bless her, good little Joanie—Although she is sleeping in the same bedroom with a man, they are not in the same bed, and that makes all the difference in the world—So, everything is honky dory?' Is that what your folks would say? Will you get accolades just because you are not in the same bed? No way. If you are in the same room, how much worse is it, in the opinion of your parents, if you are in the same bed? You have already signed a contract for a year's lease. You've already crossed the Rubicon. There's no turning back. Either your folks are clueless about everything, or they will assume the worse. There's no in between. So, a half measure at this point would be, well, pointless… Besides, wouldn't it be great to be lined up in bed like a litter of puppies?"

Joanie stared blankly. Slowly a smile spread across her face as she said, "puppies."

Mary Jane shook her head, thinking, {*All of the logic in the world was meaningless. It was the image of puppies that swayed Joanie. Heretofore, I shall invoke the idea of puppies whenever I construct an argument to persuade Joanie.*}

Joanie proclaimed, "I want an end spot, too. I get up a lot at night to go to the bathroom." She stood and said, "Excuse me." She glanced at Angelin and slightly jerked her head as an indication for Angelin to follow her to the restroom. But Angelin did not notice the summons. Joanie cleared her throat and jerked her head again.

Angelin received the message, but objected, "I just went to the pot. I don't need to go again."

Joanie's eyes bulged as she cleared her throat like the starter on the engine of a diesel truck. Angelin sighed as she stood up and followed Joanie to the restroom. It was hard to know the reason Joanie wanted Angelin to accompany her. Perhaps she wanted a private consultation with Angelin. Or just as likely, Joanie may have wanted someone to escort her to, and stand vigil over, a strange restroom. Joanie rarely went potty alone.

Mary Jane said to me, "You noticed that Joanie did not ask me to join her."

"I am sorry that you three did not develop into bosom buddies. Joanie and Angelin ran together as pups even long before I met them."

"That's OK, Daniel. I am satisfied enough."

"How about the sleeping arrangements, Mary Jane? There are only two side-ends to the bed, and Angelin and Joanie are laying claim to them. If you do not make a stink, you will end up in the middle."

"…Which is coincidentally the same place where …" Mary Jane paused, looked me in the eyes and gave the subtlest Mona Lisa smile.

જ્જ્જ્

On the way home, I had my first flat tire while driving a car, rather than a bicycle. The spare tire had a not-so-slow leak, so we limped to the first service station we could find to purchase a new inner tube. None of the girls wanted to hang around the grimy, noisy garage while the car was being serviced, so they walked across the street to a small park. Les triplés followed a path in the park that led to the back entrance of a cemetery. There were a lot of cars parked throughout the cemetery. Mostly old people were carrying plastic flowers to set at the grave sites. A casket waited for burial beside a mound of dirt from a recent excavation. The polished brass, or perhaps stainless steel, casket reflected the waning sun.

Mary Jane crossed her arms and shuddered. "This place is creepy," she muttered.

Joanie made the sign of the cross and asked, "Haven't you ever been to a cemetery before?"

"Once, when I was much younger," Mary Jane replied reflectively. A squirrel gnawed on an acorn while perched upon a small, tilted slab of an old headstone, so weathered that its inscription was no longer readable. "None of this makes any sense. The ancient Egyptians were at least consistent when it came to burials. They intended to preserve the body in the belief that the body would be used in an afterlife somewhere. They embalmed the body. Then they placed the body in a pyramid built above ground in a desert which has low humidity. In contrast, what I see here is so inconsistent. We spend a lot of money having the body embalmed at a funeral parlor. We encase the corpse in a luxurious casket. And then, in a humid area of the country, the casket is buried under ground, the most inhospitable environment for the preservation of flesh."

"You guys are giving me the hives," Angelin huffed as she dug her nails into the skin on her arms and scratched.

"Look around," Mary Jane entreated. "Even the tombstones cannot weather this climate."

"Today, I think they are called memorials, not tombstones," Joanie said.

Angelin and Mary Jane frowned at Joanie, begging the question—and what was the relevancy of Joanie's interjection?

Joanie swallowed and explained, "Well, a couple of months ago, back at school, Kazik told me about his date with Joyce, you know, the girl who lives up above—by the school bus stop?"

"Yeaaah?" chorused Angelin and Mary Jane.

"Joyce's dad is in the tombstone business. Well, when Kazik went to pick up Joyce for the date, Joyce introduced him to her folks. Kazik felt compelled to engage in conversation just to show that he was a regular guy and not a sex fiend who was taking their daughter out. Of course, we all know that that is exactly the type of guy Kazik is. Anyway, just to make conversation, Kazik asks, 'So, how is the tombstone business?' Joyce glanced sideways, nodded and said, 'They're called memorials.' 'Oh,' a wide-eyed Kazik said while nodding with scholarly demeanor."

"That's it," Angelin huffed. "The car's gotta be finished by now."

As les triplés turned to go, a cemetery worker wearing an overall bib drove by on a small tractor pulling a wagon. As the tractor passed each grave, the worker leaned sideways, extended an arm, and grabbed the plastic flowers from the base of the headstone. He chucked the plastic flowers into the wagon trailing him, including the flowers that had been delivered a mere ten minutes earlier.

Chapter XXVI

Joanie's attention deficit seemed to be getting worse. It became increasingly more difficult for her to maintain an in-depth conversation on one topic. At times, she muttered to herself incessantly, revealing the depths of her confusion for all to notice. She would digress suddenly. Often the digression bore no relationship to the topic under discussion. Joanie changed a subject in mid-sentence. Listening to Joanie was like looking towards a light source through a binoculared viewer of film negatives, mounted on a disc, showing disconnected pictures while Joanie's finger was on the slide selection crank, haphazardly flicking from scene to scene. Sometimes, she would digress four times within a period of a minute, rendering the listener baffled and increasingly irritated. Particularly irritating was Joanie's equivocation. The other day, Joanie said, "There's a blackbird on the fence. Well, it's not totally black. It has some white spots. It has a lot of white spots. There's actually more white than black. In ways it's more of a white bird." Joanie referred to an apartment as small and spacious. A person was mean and kind… Listeners were frustrated with Joanie and angry at themselves for wasting so much time listening to such babble.

Joanie's forgetfulness rendered her unable to think of a useful modifying word to complete a thought. She often talked about a person or event using a serious tone that enticed the listener with the promise of important and revealing information, only to be disappointed. As Joanie's mental focus deteriorated during her discourse, she would finish by saying, "He's really…something. He's…he's…different." Angelin said she wished Joanie would never again say the word *different*. Angelin wished Joanie would use more descriptive modifiers, such as green, or Ukrainian, raspy-voiced or ambidextrous.

Angelin felt embarrassed for Joanie when Joanie entered a group conversation without a sufficient understanding of the topic. Joanie much wanted to participate in discussions. But sometimes she would hear only two, maybe three, words and would try to divine the context of the conversation on that basis alone. She would dive into conversation with comments so out of context that others became embarrassed. Frequently, Joanie's comments sufficiently interrupted the flow of the conversation that they caused the group to lose the focus of the topic, resulting in gradual disbandment of the group.

It is hard to develop a deep relationship with someone who forgets poignant moments together. It is impossible to be soul mates with someone who forgets important parts of books or movies or the fact that she had even seen the movie at all. How can a person make insightful analysis when she cannot even keep the facts straight? It is also impossible to become a soul mate with a person of lesser intelligence. With a soul mate, you cannot wait to see her to share with her your recent discoveries about the nature of the peculiarities in your life. However, it seems pointless, and a waste of time, to share your thoughts with a person who lacks the ability to understand and appreciate ideas.

Everyone liked Joanie and wanted to spend time with her, but not on a full-time basis. An advantage to my commitment to multiple lovers was the minimization of annoying quirks from Joanie of which a high dosage could doom an exclusive, one-and-only-one-on-one, relationship. When I became weary of a flair-up of Joanie's attention deficit, I could subtly spend more time in the presence of Angelin or Mary Jane. After a respite, I could again enjoy Joanie's company and feel good about her. While I preferred being with les triplés, I could have imagined a life exclusively with Angelin. I certainly could have lived with Mary Jane only. However, if Joanie was my one and only girlfriend, the relationship would never have survived. My thoughts of Joanie were warm and positive because ninety percent of the time I was experiencing her many great traits. I did not feel trapped by her occasional, intellectual shortcomings because there was more to my life than just Joanie. Les triplés saved the relationship between Joanie and me. Everyone in the world is searching for the perfect mate … for good reason. If everyone is expecting relationship satisfaction from only one person, then that person better be creative, brilliant and damned nearly flawless. No one member of les triplés needed to meet that standard because they, in combination, exceeded perfection.

ᘒᘒᘒ

Most of the guests at Marna Sweitzer's party were acting like they were terrifically bored as a way to demonstrate their sophistication, as if you can actually be sophisticated at age eighteen. I was in a circle of former classmates who had started talking about favorite actors, which was a topic I liked. But the topics bizarrely metamorphosed into a discussion on religion. I knew that I was doomed to be drawn into the abyss. And it happened when Hank Davis, a protestant, asked me, "So, what's this thing with Catholics and the Virgin Mary?"

"It's the *Blessed* Virgin Mary, fella," I replied. "She is the quintessential mother succoring a believer to her bosom. It is all part of the radical makeover in the personality of God from the Old Testament. The paintings of the Old Testament God were of a big, muscular, powerful guy who looked like he was always angry. His face was a mixture between Thor and John Brown. He spent most of his time preserving his power and testing people's loyalty. The old God was not just omnipresent, omniscient and omnipotent; he was also omni-egotistical. What egomaniac would tell a father to kill his son for no other reason than as a sign of loyalty and then lead the man to believe that God really meant it all the time until it almost happens? What cruelty. That sounds like something Emperor Claudius would have done. Yet, no fundamentalist Christian (or Jew) ever admits that Jahweh was a mad bastard. The pre-makeover God spent a lot of time smiting people— plagues, floods, knocking down walls, turning people into pillars of salt. God was busy. Then Jesus comes along and theologians had to figure out some purpose for God having a son. And so, the new loving God was invented. Throughout the centuries, the image of Jesus became gentler and more loving, and even more gentler and even more loving, until Jesus started to appear effeminate. But no matter how effeminate Jesus became, the thought of a guy welcoming a believer to his bosom was gross. To succor someone to your bosom, you should have breasts—hence, the Blessed Mother. Since God is omnipotent, he probably wished that he had introduced amniocentesis a couple millennia earlier. If God wanted to convert to the loving campaign, then the nurturing image would have been more convincing if he had had a daughter … with a big bosom, rather than a stringy haired, effeminate son. If God had had a daughter, he may not have felt so compelled to subject everyone to the gruesome crucifixion scene. It also would have helped a lot if God were black. During slavery and the civil rights struggle, God could have said to the white Southern Baptists, 'Hey yo, what the hell do you think you're doing down there? You're pissing me off. I can turn you into a pillar of salt. I can do that. You don't want to honk me off.'"

I knew that for my sanity sake, I had to get away from that discussion. I saw Mary Jane sitting alone on an armrest of a couch. She appeared to be in her own world, swaying to the music from the hi-fi. "It is discourteous to the hostess to be antisocial at a party," I joked to Mary Jane.

"Do I seem standoffish to you?" Mary Jane asked.

"I am just kidding. It is alright to enjoy your own company for a while."

"Oh yea? I do not see anyone else alone. Everyone else looks like she is having fun and enjoying the company of others. Everyone appears as if she belongs. However, for some unknown reason, I feel like I am intruding, like I do not belong here. I feel like I am the only person here who is a stranger. I hate going to parties. They depress me. In a house of conviviality, I am an alien. I am shunned. I am alone."

"But Mary Jane, you are intellectually superior to everyone in this room."

"Even if that is true, intellectual superiority does not alleviate emotional and psychological insecurity. Intellectual self-absorption enhances alienation from others."

"Every brilliant mind has to be a little eccentric, sometimes very eccentric."

"Daniel, promise me that you will never leave me."

"I promise, Sweetheart, we will always be together."

જાજાજ

When driving home from the party, I first dropped off Joanie and then Angelin. I drove into my family's garage with Mary Jane still in the car. We started making out which escalated into an all-out encounter in lovemaking. The great thing about lovemaking is that during the climax, one's troubles are completely forgotten, albeit temporarily. It was impossible for Mary Jane to feel alienation while she was having an orgasm. Afterwards, I gave her a massage. Briefly after good sex, there is a serene feeling that everything is OK. No radical choice has to be made, no change is necessary.

Since I needed to refill the gas tank for my dad, I drove the car out of the garage and parked along the curb outside of Mary Jane's house. I walked her to the front door where I gave Mary Jane a long passionate kiss. We accentuated the sense of touch by lightly sliding our hands and arms over each other's as we swayed to imaginary music. I returned to the car and pulled away from the curb, but abruptly hit the brakes. I left the car idling in the middle of the street as I sprang from it and ran to Mary Jane who was still standing outside of the front door. I embraced and lifted her off of her feet as we kissed again.

જાજાજ

Angelin's car was more accurately the communal car of les triplés, with me bearing the burden of maintenance. The exhaust system was deteriorated in multiple spots. I was glad when my dad offered to help me replace the exhaust system because I had never before replaced one. A half hour into the job, I knew that I had again made a mistake in having him help me. Do not get me wrong, my dad was a mechanical genius. But his perfectionism dragged every job into extra hours.

Worse yet, he was the worst teacher in the world. He never said, "Here, you try it." He knew exactly what he wanted to do, and he did it— himself, while I idly stood by and watched. I suppose I should have asked for more participation on my part. But at age eighteen, it never occurred to me to request hands-on experience. He would sometimes point to something and make a comment, to which I replied, "Uh huh." But from my distant observation point, I seldom could see the object of his explanation. So, my dad worked, and I idly stood by, or sat, or kneeled. I have never been so bored in my entire life as when I stood idly for hours watching my dad play cars. I longed to leave, but how could I? After all, my dad was expending his time and effort to help *me*. If I had spent the idle hours gainfully employed doing what I knew how to do for my customers, I could have earned double the amount it would have cost to have taken the car to a service garage to have someone else fix it. The only things I learned from my dad were those that I could visually observe him doing and which I might later attempt on my own on a trial-and-error basis. I am not saying that my lack of learning mechanics was my dad's fault, and it was not my fault. We just did not connect.

Chapter XXVII

Between classes, I sat on a stone bench along the tree-lined edge of the lawn behind the Cathedral of Learning of the University of Pittsburgh. From behind me, I heard Joanie calling to me. "Were you daydreaming?" Joanie asked. "You seemed like you were in another world."

"I was in another world, fifteenth-century Greenland."

"How is fifteenth-century Greenland?"

"Cold, too cold," I answered. "The Vikings migrated to Greenland sometime before 1000 A.D. They were in Greenland for five hundred years, until the Viking population died out sometime in the 1500's."

"What killed them?" Joanie asked.

"During the five hundred year colonization, the average temperature of Greenland dropped three degrees Fahrenheit."

"That's it, only a three degree drop?"

"The name, Greenland, was an example of tenth-century false advertising. The newly arrived Vikings wanted more Vikings to come to that frozen, inhospitable place. So, they gave it the misnomer, Greenland. When the Vikings first arrived, the climate hovered precariously at the edge of survivability. The three degree drop in temperature pushed the Vikings into extinction in Greenland. The Vikings imported typical European farm animals, like cows and sheep. Archeological excavations revealed that, in the last few years, the Vikings kept the farm animals inside their homes to enhance the animals' survival."

"So, why are you thinking about the rise and fall of the Vikings in Greenland?" Joanie asked.

"Here is what fascinates me, if I could go back in time to the fifteenth century in Greenland, I would have the knowledge that could have saved a race of people on the largest island in the world. I am not talking about using the wee-wow technology available today. I mean that I could have saved the Vikings by applying the technology available in Europe during the fifteenth century. The technology of the fifteenth century for which Greenland could have most benefited would have been glassmaking. I could have taught them to array panes of glass in a latticework along the south facing walls of their earthen huts and animal shelters to provide solar heating. The glass did not have to be high quality. It did not have to be clear. It could have had bubbles and warped flaws. The only important attribute was that the glass had to permit infusion of sunlight into the enclosed living space. Later, I could have shown them how to make solar greenhouses within which the Vikings could have grown high protein and high caloric crops like beans, peas, grains and potatoes. The use of existing glassmaking technology and applying it to create solar heated environments would have made Viking survivability independent of the harsh Greenland climate. If I was there, I could have created a prosperous society in that frozen wasteland."

Kazik, a classmate of Joanie and me back at Kiski High, joined us at the bench. He was so glad to see us that he kissed Joanie on the cheek. From his book bag Kazik pulled a challah bread wrapped in wax paper. His mum had delivered it when visiting Kazik that morning. He partially unwrapped the challah and held the loaf for us each to break off a braid. "Joanie bakes challah," I said.

"You are blessed in so many ways, Daniel," Kazik said, referring to les triplés.

Joanie said, "Your mum makes good challah. The poppy seed sprinkled on the crust is a nice touch. I will try that next time I bake."

Two men wearing yarmulkes strolled along the slate-laid walkway aligning our bench. The younger man was our age and obviously a student. The older man looked like the boy's father. They were the first Jews I had ever seen. The younger man gestured and said in American English, "Look Papa, there is a challah."

Holding the wrapped end, Kazik tendered the challah, saying, "Please try some Polish bread."

The young man looked puzzled. The father's face turned ashen as he seized the son's arm. The father spoke brusquely to his son in a language I did not understand. The only word spoken that I understood was "polak".

I had a flashback to when I was a little boy at my grandparents' cottage at Pymatuning Lake. Having returned from fishing, I entered the cottage and sat down at the kitchen table to have lunch. I was still wearing my fishing hat. Babci said in a mocking and pejorative tone, "You sit at the table with hat on? What are you—Jew?"

I did not know what a Jew was. I just knew I did not want to be one. I had been conscripted into a commitment of enmity against a people whom I had never seen from an old country from which I had never been. I looked at a painted picture of the Last Supper on the wall made of glazed porcelain. I asked, "Aren't all of those men Jews? They are sitting at a kitchen table. How come they are not wearing hats?"

Babci was standing across the table from me. She had a huge knife in hand that she was using to cut bread. She leered at me. I looked at Babci and the knife in her hand. I cowered. With eyes bulging, Babci pointed to the glazed porcelain with the fingers of her other hand as she proclaimed, "Those are not men."

"They aren't?" I whispered to myself. I looked at the picture in amazement as I thought to myself that Catholic women in the days of the bible must have worn beards.

"This is Jesus," Babci said while making the sign of the cross, "and Jesus' disciples. They are all good Catholics." Babci made another sign of the cross.

I did not ask any more questions, though, because I sensed that the time had passed when I should have just shut up. After I removed my hat, Babci observed an engine grease streak across my cheek. She drew a rag from a pocket in her button-down sweater. She spat on the rag and wiped clean the grease mark. Even as a little kid, I hated when she did that.

Kazik pointed to a coed on the lawn engaged in a game of throwing a tennis ball to be retrieved by a dog. "What do you think of her?" Kazik asked.

"What do you mean—what do we think?" Joanie replied.

"What do you think of her looks—you know, her attractiveness?"

Joanie shrugged, "She's kind of masculine, yet handsome. I guess OK."

"And you, Daniel?" Kazik surveyed.

"Average, maybe a five. But since she plays catch with her dog, I will adjust the rating up to a six. What kind of a dog is that? It looks like a small bear."

"That's an old English sheepdog," Kazik replied. "That's what she told me on Monday when I asked her. She comes here most afternoons to play with that dog. Tell me, Joanie, am I any good looking?"

Joanie chuckled as she replied, "Yea, Kazik, you're good looking. I would say that you're handsome. Did you go to the prom? I didn't see you there."

"No, I never made it to the prom."

"I wish I had known you needed a date," I said. "I could have set you up with Angelin Bugliese. She was already in college then but would have liked to have returned for one more prom."

Kazik grimaced and shrugged while he said, "That's OK." His body language said, {*Are you kidding—all that dough just to be seen with a dog like her—no thanks.*} Kazik returned to the matter involving the girl with the dog. "Don't you think a plain looking girl like that would be thrilled to have a handsome guy like me show an interest in her?"

"Did you hit on her, Kazik?" Joanie asked.

"Yes, I did."

"And?"

"She got pissed off," Kazik said. Joanie and I burst into laughter. "Well, if that's how you're going to treat me, I'll just take my challah and go."

"Oh no," Joanie moaned. "Don't take away the challah. You can go, but please leave the challah bread."

"Why was she upset?" I asked.

"She said that playing with her sheepdog was a very special time for her and how dare I disturb her special moment." Kazik ripped another knot from the loaf and shook it at us to add emphasis to his words. "I have such admiration for women and their ability to reject a man's overtures when everything does not feel exactly perfect. I am especially amazed when a woman makes such a rejection when her alternative is to be totally alone. That woman causes me to ask—does a woman choose to be alone because she believes that she could quickly and easily do better than the man available, or is long-term solitude a reasonably satisfactory alternative to her?"

ॐॐॐ

Kazik got lucky a week later, scoring a movie date with an older woman (twenty something) who was a hotel receptionist. While sitting in the theater, waiting for the film to start, Esther asked, "What was it about me that made you want to ask me out?"

Kazik hated the question, but maneuvered away from a direct answer by countering with a reply question, "Why did you accept?"

"No fairs, I asked first."

Kazik made a sweeping gesture with his hand as he said, "I have been infatuated with you for years."

"But we just met."

"You did not know me, but I knew you through your riveting novel, *Moon Over Galicia*. It touched my soul. I knew that my life would not be fulfilled unless we met."

"But I never wrote a book."

"You never wrote *Moon Over Galicia*?"

"No, I never wrote any book."

"You are not Esther Frohlmann?"

"No, I'm Esther Furman."

"Oh shit! I think I've made a big mistake. I guess we will have to make the best of it, even though you have no distinguishing quality and there is no compelling reason for me to have asked you out. Now, what was it about me that enticed you to agree to go out with me?"

Chapter XXVIII

Les triplés and I had to make adjustments while living together. Fastidious Joanie insisted that we remove our shoes at the entrance to the apartment and exchange our street shoes for slippers which were kept in a milk crate at the doorway. Joanie and Angelin also wanted me to sit on the toilet seat, like a girl, when I had to go. At first, I balked at such an emasculating idea that would have me pee like a girl. But after some practice, I had to admit that sitting on the toilet like a girl was much less messy. Splashing is bound to occur when a guy goes while standing. Albeit, I would not sit on the seat at the restroom of a trucker's stop, but I sat at our private bathroom in the apartment. The sitting-like-a-girl technique made so much sense that I was amazed that no one in my family, with so many females, had insisted upon it back home.

✥✥✥

Angelin was waiting for a phone call from the University's Financial Aid Office concerning her appeal for more money. Professors had received letters from the Registrar to not let her attend classes due to non-payment of fees. Angelin was anxious to resolve the problem quickly because she had two important classes that afternoon that she had to attend. She gazed with disgust at the four bleeding fingers, where she had brutally and unrelentingly picked at her cuticles. Angelin said to herself, "I need to develop healthier habits, like smoking."

Angelin answered the phone on the first ring, "Hello."

"May I speak to Angelin Bugliese?" the caller asked.

"I am she."

"Good morning Angelin, I am Trudy Smith, and I want to tell you about the fabulous new Miracle Food Machine. It slices, it dices—no more crying over chopped onions…"

Angelin lowered the receiver and leered at it. She raised the receiver to hang up with a slam. However, she hesitated. Again bringing the receiver to her head, Angelin said in a low monotone, "Miracle Food Machine—my eye, I know who you are."

"No, Ma'am, actually we've never met."

"I surprised you by answering the phone, didn't I? You didn't expect to hear my voice."

"Ma'am?"

"You're sleeping with him, aren't you? And you don't even care that he's married with three kids at home."

"Sleeping with who?"

"You mean sleeping 'with whom', you stupid whore. You thought you could steal him away just because I gained a few pounds. Well, this is baby fat—my reward for bearing him three sons."

"Oh no, Ma'am, you're making a mistake. I'm not sleeping with no one. I sell the fabulous Miracle Food Machine with five patented attachments. My supervisor will be coming back from lunch in just a minute, and she can explain …"

"Bullshit, Trudy, I know you're sleeping with him. Why don't you just admit it, you harlot?"

"No, Ma'am!"

"Then, how do you know my name?"

"It's on the list. I have a list here, and my supervisor …"

"I know where you live, Trudy."

"Ma'am, I'm hanging up now."

"Don't you hang up on me, you bitch."

෨෨෨

The job of working the reserve desk of the law library was perfect for me to catch up on homework or to catnap, if I needed it. I sometimes worked the main law library on the fourteenth floor of the Cathedral of Learning. Most of the time, though, I worked evenings until closing in the auxiliary law library for the first-year law students located on the fifth floor. The fifth floor room was huge with hand carved tables and chairs. Usually, no one showed up, which was fine by me. I believed that the primary purpose for the fifth floor library was to store second copies of treatises that no one used nor wanted. All of the books were kept downstairs, not on the fourth floor, but rather on shelves arrayed on a false floor dangling from cables suspended underneath the fifth floor. The suspended floor clanked with a metal sound and swayed when walked upon, like a bridge catwalk or an amusement park spook house. With a low ceiling and illumination by only a few naked twenty-five watt light bulbs, floor four-and-a-half was a dark, creepy netherworld. During a 6 PM-to-11PM stint in the fifth floor library for 1L's, the room was vacant, except for one female student who had books and papers strewn over a table, eight feet in length. For an hour the 1L shuffled from book to book to notepad, furiously rustling through pages. She tilted her head to a side and draped her arms around her head. She squeezed her head until there was a popping sound, like a person cracking his knuckles. But she did it to her neck. I had never before seen anyone do that. It sounded like she had broken her frick'n neck. She threw down her pencil, stood up and walked to the reserve desk. The 1L stiff-armed the desk and leaned forward as she said, "Look, kid, I have a project that's going to take me all night to finish."

"Yes, Ma'am?"

"And I'm too keyed up to concentrate."

"Yes, Ma'am."

"And I really need to be able to focus."

"And how can I help?"

"How old are you, kid?"

"Ma'am?"

"You know, what year are you?"

"Freshman, I am eighteen."

"Oh, for heaven's sake," the girl said as she rolled her eyes. "I need sexual satisfaction, and you are going to relieve my tension."

"Me?!" I gasped. "But … but I do not even know you." I scanned her features. Her face was plain. Her body was plain …It was OK. But what mattered most was that she was female and would have the scent of a female.

"Look, kid, there's no time to argue. I'm on a tight deadline, and this is going to happen." The 1L surveyed the room and focused on the stairwell to the suspended netherworld. "Down there, we'll do it down there."

"Down in the hole? Have you ever been down there? It is creepy. It is quite dusty, too."

"I'm not going to lie down," the girl said.

"Well then, like, how do we do it?"

"You mean—how do you do it. While I hold onto a book case, you will kiss my neck. You will then kiss my back and work your way down to my ass. And then you will perform orally on me."

"And for me, what do I get? Are you going to reciprocate on me?"

"Oh no, that would gag me. I'm not doing anything, except slipping down my panties."

"That is not fair," I protested.

"You will experience a fantasy that you can recall a thousand times whenever you are bored with someone else. For now, you can just satisfy yourself. Take it or leave it."

∂∂∂

When the 1L and I returned to the fifth floor, I voiced regret over my infidelity. The girl scoffed at my concern and demanded that I answer her question, "What is my name?"

"I do not know your name," I replied.

"I rest my case. You cannot be guilty of infidelity if you do not even know my name."

"Who made that rule?" I begged.

"It's the common law of contacts, kid. Besides, you are an employee of the Law School. You have a duty to facilitate the educational process. I was so hyped that my educational process came to a halt. Your Johnny-on-the-spot has enabled me to go back to that table and bang out a first-rate brief… By the way, kid, you need to wash your face."

Chapter XXIX

"Oh my God, oh no, what am I going to do?!" Joanie cried as she circled the living room, pressing the palms of her hands against her forehead.

"What's wrong?" Angelin asked. She had been underlining key phrases of a chapter in a textbook while sprawled out on a bench made of blankets spread over boards supported by cinderblocks.

"Where's Daniel?" Joanie demanded. "You guys got me into this mess. Now, you have to get me out of it."

Hearing the commotion from the hallway as I returned from collecting the mail, I entered the apartment and sayeth, "Why dost thou take my name in vein?"

"My folks—my whole family—are coming to visit."

"So what's the problem? You just meet them in the lobby of Holland Hall," Angelin said.

"They are coming early so that I can give them a tour of the University. My mom wants to see my dorm room. And then they want to have lunch in the cafeteria. What am I gonna do?"

"Joanie, call your mum back and tell her that the residence management will not allow non-residents to go up to the suites in the women's dorms," I suggested.

"That's ridiculous, Daniel," Angelin chided. "Just how naïve do you think our parents are?"

"Look," I said, "if they want to see a dorm room, then show them a dorm room—any dorm room. Show them Marna's room. I will get her number." I bolted towards the bedroom and ran into the walk-in closet. Retrieving the tablet of vital statistics from my backpack, I looked up the number for Marna Schweitzer's suite in Holland Hall. I showed Joanie the number, and she dialed it.

A person answered, saying, "Won yong shee jang."

"Excuse me," Joanie said, "Is this Holland Hall? … Oh, I'm sorry, I must have dialed the wrong number." Joanie frantically hung up and said, "This is the wrong frick'n number."

"I have used that number a hundred times." I snatched the receiver and dialed Marna's suite, "Good morning. Is Marna there? Oh, oh geez … no, no message. Sorry for waking you up on a Saturday morning. Bye." I hung up and reported, "She went home for the weekend, boyfriend problems."

"I'm doomed."

I looked desperately at Angelin who said, "The cafeteria is no problem. Somehow we can get lunch tickets for everyone. Daniel, you take care of that. Now, a dorm room? There are thousands of dorm rooms. We just have to get one girl to let us use her room for half an hour."

"Who?" Joanie asked with a slight showing of confidence in Angelin's manifestation of determined authority.

Angelin turned to me and demanded, "Give me five bucks. No, make it ten dollars."

"For what?"

"You are going to give me ten bucks because you don't want me to rip your lips off of your face." I gave Angelin ten dollars. Angelin turned to Joanie and instructed, "Get your suitcase and fill it with some personal things your mom and sister will recognize, like that fuzzy dog with the torn ear and the ratty, threadbare pajamas you like. Don't forget your rosary and that picture of the Sacred Heart of Jesus with the eyes that follow you around the room."

We did a speed walk for the mile to the dorms. The suitcase was awkward for Joanie to lug at so quick a pace, so I carried it for her on my head, like a Ubangi woman from the African bush. Angelin and Joanie turned into the quad of the women's dorms, while I continued towards the three, twenty-two story, round towers of men's dorms.

Under the men's towers was a cafeteria. I went to the towers residence management desk and asked to purchase seven lunch tickets for visitors.

"May I see your meal pass." the part-time clerk requested. He obviously was a student.

"Okie Dokie," I said as I rummaged through my backpack as if I were looking for my meal pass. Of course, I did not have a meal pass because I was not a dorm resident. While using my right hand to pretend looking through my book bag, I slid my left hand into my pants pocket, wherein I slipped my little finger through a key ring that had one key attached. I slid the hand out of the pocket and placed it on the top of the book bag, with the key ring and key dangling prominently from the little finger. The key caught the eye of the student clerk. It was a typical Pitt key, similar to the thousands of dorm keys. However, unbeknownst to the clerk, the key was to the lock on the door to the reserve book room in the Law Library on the fourteenth floor of the Cathedral of Learning, where I worked part-time.

Believing the key to be a dorm key, the clerk waved off my effort and said, "Screw it. You said seven lunch tickets?"

"Yea."

The clerk went to the cash register and rang up, "7 lunches @ $1.15 = $8.05,"

Back at the women's quad, Angelin climbed atop a long, stone-sided flower bed, made a megaphone by cupping her hands, and broadcasted, "I have ten dollars to give to anyone to let us use your room for half an hour!" Joanie grimaced at the announcement. Many coeds were strolling across the quad. Several laughed, but none showed an interest in accepting the offer. Angelin whispered to Joanie, "I can't believe there are no takers for ten bucks."

Joanie raspily whispered back, "That's because you made it sound like we're lesbians in heat. They don't want their sheets gooed up."

"For ten bucks, I'd let two elephants go at it in my bed. Sheets can be washed." …Angelin megaphoned, "No, no, you got it wrong. We are pulling a prank on her parents, and we'll pay ten dollars to pretend to her parents that your room is hers!"

Many coeds glanced at each other, and a few stopped walking. One girl hollered back, "Ten bucks, what's the scam?"

"My friend's parents are coming to Pitt to see her suite room. The problem is—she's living in an apartment with a guy."

Giggles spread through the quad. Joanie closed her eyes and cowered. She yelled a whisper to Angelin, "Why don't you announce to God and everyone that I'm a slut?"

Angelin continued, "We just want to sprinkle a stuffed doggy and a few other artifacts around your room and have you escort her family up to your suite. She'll show them your room, as hers. They'll sit a few minutes in the living room to shoot the shit. Then, they'll go to lunch. That's it, ten bucks!"

"I'll take it," a voice proclaimed while pointing an index finger into the air.

"No, I'll do it," another coed countered. "I really need the money."

"I'll do it for nine," yelled a third.

"No," Angelin announced, "the price is ten dollars, but it's for the cleanest room." Moans rumbled through the gallery. Joanie was a clean freak when it came to anyone visiting, especially if a group of people came to the apartment. Even if just one person came to dinner, Joanie cleaned the whole apartment. Perhaps she was worried that people would not like her unless her apartment was spotless and her salads were colorfully displayed. When Angelin saw that Angelin's turn for cleaning the kitchen and bathroom would soon arrive, Angelin invited one of Joanie's friends to dinner, just so Joanie would do all of the cleaning for Angelin. Joanie was keen on others' perceptions of her. While getting ready to go out just for class, Joanie changed outfits four times before making a final choice. She was so indecisive. It was a fashion show every morning. After all the effort Joanie expended towards making a good impression, she would have been appalled to discover that the overall impression remaining with a person who had met Joanie was that she was a sweet, kind, caring, scatter-brained ditz whose words had little value.

"My room and suite are clean," a coed declared.

"Sold!" Angelin boomed with a pointed finger at the end of an extended arm.

When I arrived at the quad, I did not see Joanie or Angelin. So, I entered the Holland Hall lobby to wait for someone to check me in as a guest. A few minutes later, a girl walked out of the elevator. She surveyed the lobby and paused when she saw me. She smiled and asked with a New Jersey accent, "Are you Daniel?"

"Yes. Are Joanie and Angelin in your suite?"

"Yea."

"And Joanie is frantically cleaning it?"

The girl giggled and said, "I can't believe it. You could serve food on my floors, That's how clean they are. My name is Rosie." She extended her hand to shake. She was petite at five foot max and wore a Star of David on a necklace. "We're suppose to wait here for Joanie's family. Do you know them?"

"Yes," I replied. "In fact, they are walking across the parking lot right now. I will get them."

Rosie escorted Joanie's family up to her suite. I could have gone up to the room, but I remained in the lobby to enhance the impression that men were rarely found in the quad dorms. I pulled from my book bag a text on symbolic logic and worked on some homework problems. I liked doing symbolic logic proofs. They reminded me of solving puzzles in high school geometry using the theorems. I was so engrossed in contemplation that Angelin had to shake me to restore my sentience.

After we had surrendered our tickets and entered the cafeteria, Joanie's dad looked back at the entrance checkpoint and noticed a coed entering by merely flashing a meal I.D. card. "How come she doesn't need a ticket to get in?" Papa Slabovnyk querried.

"Oh, her?" Joanie replied. "That's … what's her face."

"Susan," Angelin stepped in with a fake name. "She's a nursing student. The nursing students have their own dorm and cafeteria where they use I.D's. They also have the option of dining in this cafeteria using their meal pass."

The girl was immediately followed by a guy who also flashed a meal pass. "What about him?" Joanie's dad asked.

"Oh, he's a nursing student, also," Angelin fired back.

"Men nurses?" Joanie's dad whispered incredulously.

"Well," Angelin replied, "there are some types of operations where you really wouldn't want a woman present." Joanie's dad grimaced.

The meal with Joanie's family went well. Angelin and I scarfed up mounds of fruit as if we had been stowed away on a scurvy infested ship. Joanie looked like she was spaced out on happy tranquilizers. Near the end of the meal, Joanie's mother turned to Joanie and said, "I hear such terrible stories about girls in college. I worry so much that I can't sleep at night."

"Ah Mummy, you can see that I am very safe here. And I have a lot of friends." Angelin and I looked up from our cornucopia and smiled broadly.

Joanie's mother drove for a home run, "I beg you to ease my mind. Swear that you have not done any bad things—that you are a virgin. Swear this on the rosary." The mother extended a fist with a rosary wrapped around her hand.

Everyone at the table froze in place. I could not believe that Joanie's mum had pleaded for reaffirmation of purity of the flesh in that godforsaken bunker thirty feet below the surface of the ground. Above us were thousands of beds that conspired on weekend nights to create a rhythmic cacophony of ka-chinka ka-chinga sounds from strained bedsprings employed in the college ritual of debauchery that made it impossible for an alone sonuvabitch to be able to get any sleep. Joanie sat silently with an expression of numbness and melancholy. Angelin and I knew that Joanie could not lie on a rosary. Just sitting there, she looked guilty as sin.

Angelin moved almost out of her seat to place her arm around Joanie's shoulders and to impose her body so far into Joanie's seated space as to protrude her head closer to Joanie's mum than Joanie's own head. Angelin said, "I agree with you, Joanie, that the request is unseemly for a girl who has spent her whole life living virtuously. But maybe, just this once, you could graciously ease your mom's anxiety and simply swear to the truth." Joanie's eyes and head slowly turned toward Angelin in horror and disbelief. Angelin continued, "As I could forthrightly bear witness, you can swear that every night in Pittsburgh you have slept with me, every night you sleep with a woman." When Joanie did not respond timely enough, Angelin smilingly dug her knuckles into Joanie's ribs and squeezed.

Joanie winced and placed her hand on the rosary and vowed, "I so swear."

Joanie's mum leapt towards her daughter and embraced her. The mother wept as she declared, "I will never doubt you again, my precious little girl."

Chapter XXX

Angelin and I walked to the front patio of the Cathedral of Learning. We sat on a stone bench that was ten yards away from a pool with a spout of water flowing from the mouth of a stone panther head. The bench was the designated spot to meet Joanie after her family left. "Maybe one of us should have stayed with Joanie to help out in case her folks ask a question to which she does not know how to answer diplomatically," I fretted.

"Give it a break, Daniel. I'm getting tired of Joanie's double life. Honestly, I wish her family would learn the truth so that the charade would end."

"But you have not been totally straight with your folks either."

"Yea, but I'm a much better liar than Joanie. If I had to have gone through half of this shit, I would've fessed up. At least I have told them the truth that I'm living in an apartment with Joanie."

"Thank God," I said. "If your folks come down, you can show them the apartment."

"Yea, then all we would need is for you to move all your stuff out." As my jaw dropped, Angelin chuckled and added, "I'm just pulling your cord. There's no way my dad is going to drive into Pittsburgh. As long as I visit them occasionally at home, we're safe."

"Where is Joanie? What time is it?"

"Ya'know, Joanie has been getting on my nerves lately."

"Why?" I asked.

"Do you remember that Lebanese restaurant where I asked to be seated away from the screaming kid? Joanie's been giving me all this grief about my not having a maternal instinct and that I would be a terrible mother. So, what do you think?" Angelin asked. "Do you think I would be a bad mother?"

"No, that is ridiculous. You will make a terrific mom."

"She also thinks that you are insensitive."

"Joanie always slips over the edge when the topic of babies and families comes up," I said. "She is riddled with anxiety because the status of les triplés is not leading her to either. She may someday fly the coup. I know not to where she will fly. I just know that pressure grows within her, like magma in a volcano."

"How do you feel about that—you know—about babies and families? Do you want to be a parent someday?"

"A parent? No and yes."

"For God's sake," Angelin huffed, "you're starting to sound as equivocal as Joanie."

"I do not want to be a father. I know that much for sure. Rather, I want to be a mother."

"Okie dokie," Angelin said while pursing her lips. "That's pretty weird, seeing that you are male."

"Just look at my dad. As a father, all my dad is is a provider. I am not saying that being a provider is a bad thing, but that is all he does. He works hard. He works overtime to make more money for his large family. He works long hours maintaining the house. He fixes everything. I have never seen a broken appliance or gadget that he could not fix. And I admire him for that. But the problem with my dad is that he does not have a relationship … with anyone. He is like a worker bee who keeps hauling in the pollen, but he seldom talks to anyone back in the hive. The biggest mistake a provider makes is in his expectation that providees will love him in exchange for his diligence in providing. A provider may possibly believe that it is part of a divine contract—he busts his ass, and you love him for it. But it does not work that way. No one ever loved a provider for the mere fact that he is a provider. The only regard a providee has for a provider is the expectation that the provider will keep on providing, and that is all. Most providees disrespect the provider. It is depressing to see provider-fathers so devoted during their entire lives to such unfulfilling projects. I wish this were not so, but I believe it to be true. Although I am an atheist, I hope for my dad's sake that there really is a God because if there is no God, then when it comes to cosmic justice, I fear that my dad is really going to be screwed. He has spent his whole life making massive deposits of faith and unselfish self-sacrifice into God's bank only to find the account bankrupt when he dies."

"But you also have the traits of a provider," Angelin noted.

"If I have inherited that from my dad, then I thank him because I think an altruistic sense of duty to help is a good thing. But, most importantly, you do not stay with me just because I provide you with food and an apartment," Angelin stared at me with a cross between her poker face and Mona Lisa.

I continued, "My mum has relationships … with her daughters, but not with my brother and me. Sometimes my sisters will have a conversation about events that happened years ago. Each will nod her head acknowledging her familiarity with the story, a story of which I had never heard. The only history of my family of which I am aware, especially about my mother, I have learned through eavesdropping on my sisters' conversations with each other. In the family solar system, my mum is the sun. My sisters are the closest planets. And my dad, God love him, is like Pluto way out there—not having any gravitational effect on the tides."

"And what are you, Daniel?"

"I am Uranus. My sisters constantly draw comparisons between me and my dad, and also my grandfather for that matter. To the extent the comparison includes their hard work, frugality and commitment, I accept the analogy as a compliment. However, I could not survive one day in the emotional desert in which my dad exists. So, do I want to be a father? Instinctively, I realize I could not be a father in a traditional, monogamous relationship. I could imagine having a close, one-on-one, relationship with a woman without having children. But I would fear that childbirth would also bring me banishment to the emotional desert on Pluto. The cycle of male estrangement continued. I would be my father. I shall never let that happen. I do not have to be the one and only element in the nucleus of my life, but I absolutely shall be an essential part of the nucleus.

Angelin stood up and stretched her arms over her head. She went over to an adjacent flowerbed and smelled a rose. Shaking her head, she said, "And to think that all this time I thought les triplés was an accidental freak in the history of human relationships. Now, I realize that it was bound to happen. Your inherent predisposition drove you, and you drove all of us, to where we are today. I always thought that all of this was your fault. Now I know that all of this is your fault."

"I never contemplated a concept like les triplés," I said. "How could I have conceived of something I had never seen before?"

"It was so obvious. Before Mary Jane's face turned into strawberry preserves, you were really hot for her."

"I am still really hot for her."

"Yet when she presented the ultimatum, you chose the option that risked losing her in exchange for the greatest probability of preserving les triplés, at least two out of three."

"Methinks you give me way too much credit. It is more plausible that I simply lacked the balls to make a choice. Mary Jane left us as a default resulting from my paralysis."

"I bet that if Mary Jane had not returned, you would have replaced her."

I laughed. "Just like that, you and Joanie would have accepted a new girl at the time when we were in high school? And can you think of another girl in high school who would have been willing to accept such an arrangement? You do not appreciate how fragile les triplés has been. It was tough enough initiating les triplés when we were innocent, naive kids who were just being friends. I carefully maintained a balance of attention among you. And yet, the relationship almost unraveled a couple of times. Look at the world; do you see anything like les triplés out there?"

"There have been harems before," Angelin retorted.

"Les triplés is not a harem. We all assent to it. Harems never involved assent and consent of the women. Rich, powerful guys bought or just took the women. You are overreaching, Angelin. Look at the thousands of people in our world, in this city, or back at Kiski. They consider us freaks. Have you ever seen anything like les triplés? I never have. As far as I can see, les triplés is unique."

"If les triplés is such an oddity—indeed, unique as you would say—then is it a good thing? Could something so unnatural be good?"

"I do not think that les triplés is unnatural. It is un-normal. But I think it is perfectly natural for me. You said that you thought that I would have replaced Mary Jane if she had not returned. I think you are right because we both know that that is my nature. While I question the probability for success for attempting to add another life partner as late as our high school years, I would have died trying. During an age of rampant divorce among monogamous couples, les triplés works because of the consummate commitment to it. I am not a potentate in control of a harem. Quite to the contrary; you girls are in control of me. Regardless of her qualities, no one woman in a monogamous relationship with me could satisfy my emotional needs. I am fully aware of the uniqueness of les triplés and of just how lucky I am. Today, it would be impossible to replicate les triplés from scratch. I have attained my emotional potential. You must know that I am committed to you for life."

"Yes, Daniel, we know that."

"But to answer your question of whether les triplés is a good thing, I think you need to answer a simple question; are you happy?"

Angelin grinned and replied, "I am happy, but I think I could be happier."

"What would it take?"

"On Tuesday and Thursday mornings, Joanie has a nine a'clock class. Instead of you taking a shower early like you normally do, can you wait until she leaves for class?"

"Yea."

"And then you can take a shower with me?"

"Yea."

"Can you shampoo my hair into a big lather—I mean a really big lather?"

"Yea."

"Can you spread the suds over my back?"
"Yea."
"And over my breasts?"
"Yea."

Chapter XXXI

The good townspeople of Vandergrift stare at us as we stroll through Jackson Park during the Labor Day festivities. My daughter, Moira, sucks on a toy as I carry her papoose-style. Her mother, Mary Jane, carries a tote bag with its straps slung over her left shoulder. The bag contains bottles of formula, bottles of water, and diapers. Angelin pushes Tamera in a stroller. Tamera is three months old and three weeks junior to her half-sister, Moira. Joanie slides her hand around my inner elbow and holds on as we stroll. I look up at two clouds merging in a blue, sun-drenched sky. I am the happiest man alive.

"Do I show?" Joanie whispers self-consciously.

"Of course not, Sweetheart," I say soothingly. "You will not start showing for another month. You know that."

"How do I explain this to my family?" Joanie laments.

Mary Jane responds, "Tell them that you joined the Peace Corp and you are spending a year in Djibouti. After the baby is delivered, you can see your folks, and they will have no idea that you had been in the family way."

"But what about the baby? They have a right to see their first grandchild."

"Tell your folks that you adopted the baby when the parents were tragically lost in a sand storm."

"I can't say that."

"Tell them she is your baby by immaculate conception."

"I can't say that."

"Why not? There is precedence."

The End

About the Author

Daniel Plucinski is a professor of Business Law at Frostburg State University. He is a CPA and a CMA (Certified Management Accountant) and earned a BA in philosophy and an MBA from the University of Pittsburgh and a J.D. from the University of Baltimore. His first novel was *I Am Not My Mother* which may be purchased by e-mail request todplucinski@frostburg.edu. Type message: "Send me a book order form."

And I shall send you a purchase order. Professor Plucinski is completing his third novel, *You Have No New Messages*.